A THYME FOR LOVE

A THYME
FOR LOVE

Celia H. Miles

For E.A.
Enjoy the story &
try the recipes

Celia Miles

ISBN 0-7414-1484-8

Published by:
INFINITY
PUBLISHING.COM
519 West Lancaster Avenue
Haverford, PA 19041-1413
Info@buybooksontheweb.com
www.buybooksontheweb.com
Toll-free (877) BUY BOOK
Local Phone (610) 520-2500
Fax (610) 519-0261

Printed in the United States of America

Printed on Recycled Paper

Published April 2003

Contents

Cary's Collection of Recipes

This book is dedicated to Yvonne Lehman, who got it started, and to my friends and fellow authors in the French Broad Writers. I especially thank Frances Payne for her encouragement and Maria Fire and Nancy Dillingham for their thoughtful reviewing.

Chapter 1

Her little red MG tilted precariously in the ditch. It would require judicious steering and someone pushing, Cary thought ruefully, to maneuver it back on the dusty gravel road. She sighed and reached for her shoulder bag. For now, she would be content to simply get herself out of the car and let someone else get the car out of the ditch. The late afternoon sun was hot, even here in the mountains of western North Carolina where misty mornings and cool evenings were the advertised speciality.

Cary swung her legs out of the low-slung vehicle and surveyed the deserted area. The road twisted and turned and headed into an opening in the mountainside. "The best-laid schemes o' mice an' men gang aft aglet," she muttered in a soft Virginian accent, "and of women too." She tended to quote poetry in moments of stress or moments of happiness—whenever it popped out. And right now, Bobby Burns' poem popped out and she finished the quotation: "An' lea'e us nought but grief an' pain for promis'd joy."

There was no way she could reach over—once she had clambered up the bank—to lock the door. But the road

certainly did not look heavily traveled, so she supposed her
luggage and camera equipment would be okay in the car.

A moment of uncertainty assailed her. What was she doing in this out-of-the-way place? Walking toward a farm somewhere up this road, a farm with a cottage for rent. Undoubtedly she should have investigated the place more fully. But
the tiny classified ad in the Norfolk paper had instantly ap-
pealed to her because it seemed to promise seclusion and
privacy. One rental cottage on a farm surely meant she wouldn't
have to mingle and socialize. She could concentrate on re-
evaluating what she wanted to do with her life.

Her directions on the phone from someone named Mary
had indicated that ThymeTable Farm was approximately two
miles from the turn off the main road, and just before she
had applied the brakes too forcefully in that blind curve,
she'd checked the odometer. She couldn't have more than
half a mile to walk. She set out, thankful that at least she'd
put on her wide brimmed sun hat. Now she took her sunglasses from her bag. Cary's sense of humor told her how
ridiculous she must look—very much the tourist. But, she
thought, I am a tourist and who's looking? A car, a pickup
truck, a bicycle even, would be welcome!

Cary's weak left foot began to throb. Darn, she thought, I
should have worn walking shoes. Any other time, Cary would
have paid close attention to the chicory blooming along the
road, its blue flowers appearing fresh even if its stalks and
leaves were dusty. She would have appreciated the photogenic possibilities of the rusty wire fence running along the
upper bank, perhaps have noticed the baby rabbit scamper-
ing away as she approached.

Today, however, she began to wonder if she'd made a
mistake coming here. She could just hear her brother Phillip
telling her that she had, that she needed people, that she
needed her family, that she needed to think through her
decision to dash off alone. Need! Cary had heard the word so

often recently that merely remembering made her anger rise. Need. Need. Need. The words tramped along with her, like soldiers marching in her head. She almost missed the turnoff, then spied a white gate standing invitingly open, and saw with relief the smoother asphalt of a paved driveway. By the gate was a sign. Blue letters on white announced: ThymeTable Farm.

Cary stopped in the shade of a large oak, which with a row of smaller trees, bordered the road. She could see her destination a few hundred feet ahead. Or at least she could see several buildings, including a cottage on her left. A large white two-story frame farmhouse sat some distance beyond. Various other buildings, including plastic covered greenhouses, were scattered over the fields.

Surveying the scene, Cary had to admit the place did have a certain charm. She looked around for any sign of life. In this idyllic setting, shouldn't a dog, a friendly collie or a spotted beagle, have come bounding out to greet her? Didn't every farm have its resident dog? ThymeTable Farm was quiet and isolated.

Or so it seemed—until Cary saw a movement, across a field, to her right. Something—no, someone bent over, intently studying the ground. Good. The man could tell her about checking in and getting help with her car. She decided to cut across the weeds to ask directions of the worker. Even if it meant saving herself some steps, even if her patience was evaporating in the heat, Cary would not yell and attract attention to herself.

Surely he would notice her, Cary thought as she stepped gingerly through the field in her elegant wedge sandals. Just as she was within a few feet of the shirtless man, close enough to note his muscular back and his muddy boots, a large flying insect zipped by her head. A small startled sound escaped her.

"Watch it! You're all over the thyme!" Hardly words of welcome, and the exasperated face of the speaker didn't look hospitable either. While she had swerved to avoid the bee or bug, the man had turned and was glaring at her.

What a way to greet a potential guest, a customer at the farm, thought Cary. And even if he is the gardener or hired hand, he could be more welcoming. After all, she had been forced to come traipsing across the field to get his attention. Surely she had every right to be annoyed, not him.

"What . . . . what about the time?" Trying to regain some composure her voice became haughty. She glanced at her watch. "I know I said I'd be here by three, but my car . . ."

The gardener grinned, his teeth white in his tanned face and a decided smudge on one cheek where he'd wiped his face. A devilish sparkle lit his amber-brown eyes. Leaning on the shovel, one hand holding a bucket of sprigs, he looked toward her feet.

"Thyme, lady. T-h-y-m-e." He spelled and waved the bucket. "You're standing in it—and on it."

Cary's face burned. As she hastily stepped out of what she'd assumed were weeds, she winced slightly with the pain in her foot.

Disregarding his questioning look, she spelled back at him crossly. "I'm sorry about the t-h-y-m-e," she apologized. "But I, um, would have expected it on a table. Right?"

She'd hoped for a touch of humor, but he surveyed the patch of thyme as if she had murdered his prize flowers or something. Well, at least this worker took pride in his labor, even if he didn't have much regard for people. For her, anyway.

She lifted her chin higher and met his eyes. Her businesslike, aloof tone didn't quite disguise the fatigue in her voice. "I'm Cary Randall. I called several days ago to say I'd be here this afternoon. Whom do I see about the cottage?"

The man dropped his shovel and placed the bucket on the ground. He rubbed his hand on his jeans. "I'm . . ." he began as he strode toward her. In her surprise Cary stepped back and again the errant foot protested. Her yelp interrupted both his movement and his introduction. She bit her lip to still the spasm of pain.

Whatever Cary expected next, it was not that the man would simply swoop down, pick her up so effortlessly and start across the field with her pressed against his chest. Her hat was knocked askew, and her shoulder bag dangled from her imprisoned arms.

"What are you doing?" Cary yelled, a somewhat muffled yell, granted, but this, this gardener had no right to assume he could—if not knock her off her feet—yank her off her feet and manhandle her this way!

"Put me down! I can walk. Put me down this minute!"

Even as she protested, Cary recognized the prudish sound of her protests, like some schoolmarm of the 1890s or something. The truth was, in his strong arms, she felt both inordinately silly and obscurely secure. She stifled a small giggle about to erupt. Maybe this kind of service came with the fee for the cottage! She might as well enjoy herself, ridiculous though she must seem. Just as she was beginning to relax, he deposited her, none too gently, on a wooden bench in front of the cottage.

Cary tried to regain some degree of dignity by removing her half-crushed hat and smoothing her hair. "Thank you very much," she said, wishing to be gracious without appearing too grateful. The man paid no attention to her. Without a word, he knelt before her and began gently removing her left sandal.

"What's wrong with it?" he asked, as he inspected her foot.

"What are you doing?" Cary responded indignantly.

The man ignored her question. His hands were deft and sure as he examined her foot. For a long moment Cary was still, wanting only to be touched, longing for his slightly roughened fingertips to play on her flesh. She studied the precise cut of his dark brown hair. It was full and heavy, swept back from his forehead and short about his ears. Cary, who prided herself on describing students at the college where she worked in quick and clever one-liners, could think of only one word to sum up the face bent over her feet: perfect. She looked more closely. But surely his jaw was a little too lean, his stubble a little heavy for early afternoon, and wasn't that a tiny scar near his left temple? Yes, practically perfect. He had the good looks she associated with Ivy League colleges, fraternities, and models for Christian Dior neckwear collections. Even in his muddy jeans, he exuded a confidence at home in boardrooms and bedrooms.

Suddenly irritated by her pleasure at his ministrations, she jerked her foot away, annoyed that she had enjoyed his gentleness and that he had assumed such, such a liberty with her.

He grinned as though he read her thoughts. Apparently satisfied that nothing was broken, he replaced her sandal and asked again, "What's with the foot? And why were you walking anyway?" He looked down the driveway for a vehicle.

"My foot is none of your business!" Cary replied pertly. "And I'm walking because my car is in a ditch!"

He grinned once more. "Well, you don't have to tell me the secret of the foot." He touched the tip of her toe. "But you should wear walking shoes for walking. You're in the country now."

"Just where do I find the owner or the manager or somebody to see about the cottage?" Cary was determined to get on with business and to put this stranger, this shirtless stranger, back in the field where he belonged. His bare chest with its dark hair glistening in the sun's rays was distracting. Around his neck a silver chain holding a silver medallion with a design both simple and obscure drew her eyes. She lowered her gaze and rummaged in her purse for a slip of paper.

The man walked over to the cottage porch and picked up a shirt draped over the railing.

"Is the owner—?" she glanced at the paper seeking the name. "Is Mr. Bradford here today?"

Tucking his chambray shirt into his jeans, the man nodded casually. "I'll show you around." He gestured toward the cottage. "This is it," he declared unnecessarily, with all the charm of a desk clerk who never intends to see the customer again. "Rosemary Cottage."

It was tidy, small, and white with green trim. Tall pines guarded its sides and a neat path led to its green door. The door stood open, in welcome. Two steps led up a narrow porch with a waist-high railing. Pots of flowers were scattered at one corner of the porch and a bench, a twin to the one she had been deposited on, occupied the other side. Obviously neither new nor newly painted, the cottage had a cozy, down-home appeal. This might be exactly what she had hoped for. She wasn't here to bask in the formal luxury in an impersonal hotel suite.

The man moved aside so she could mount the steps. Momentarily intrigued by the delicately decorated door harp, or perhaps distracted by his presence, Cary paused a shade longer than she intended. "It's . . . . neat. I'll go inside if you don't mind."

"Of course. It has all the usual modern conveniences," he said, perhaps mistaking her hesitation for disapproval. "Well, no air-conditioning, but we don't usually need it out here. Has a nice screen door."

She heard the slightly inflected sarcasm. He didn't sound like a man who'd just carried her across the field and across her protest. Cary didn't know what was bothering him or what was bothering her about him!

"The television is on the blink right now, but without cable out here, it doesn't get good reception anyway." Was he now trying to discourage her, wondered Cary. Lack of a television wouldn't deter her, if that was his intent.

As Cary opened the cottage door, he continued, "If you're one of those women who can't live without your daily dose of soap operas, this place is not for you."

"Thank you," Cary returned coolly. She took off her sunglasses and stared into his eyes. "I can live without them if I choose to . . ." At that instant, she forgot the name of every single soap opera except the one her mother was addicted to, so she finished, "all the days of my life."

He looked at her strangely.

"It—All the Days of Our Lives—is a soap opera. It's the only one I could think of." She chuckled nervously. Apparently her little attempt at humor had only been interpreted as weird. The man nodded blandly, but his mind was surely elsewhere. Probably back with his bucket and shovel.

The living room, small and warmly inviting, painted in tones of green and beige with creamy walls, had a low ceiling which boasted a fan. A stone fireplace faced the sofa, and pottery lamps, in surprisingly delicate hues, were well placed.

Muslin curtains covered with a muted green block print of what looked like Shasta daisies filtered the glare of the afternoon sun.

Cary looked around. To her left the dining area contained an oaken table surrounded by four chairs, each having a thin cushion with a repeat of the Shasta daisy print. Beyond was a small kitchen visible through the doorway.

"Bedroom's in back, with a large bathroom and closets." The man seemed less and less interested in his self-appointed task of showing her the premises. As Cary turned, she caught his quickly concealed frown. His arms were folded against his chest.

"Is the owner here?" she asked again.

"Allow me to introduce myself, Ma'am," he exaggerated the word, as if she were closer to the mid-century mark than to the quarter century! "I'm Spencer Bradford. I own ThymeTable Farm. Just call me Spence."

Cary was caught off guard. "Oh, I thought you were," she faltered for a moment, then plunged on. "I thought you were working here."

"I do work here. I'm your handyman, plumber, errand boy, and garbage collector. I can fix roofs, sinks, ovens, just about anything that breaks. I'll deliver your mail and I'll even serenade you if you so desire." He bowed with a flourish. "We aim to please at ThymeTable."

He may be trying to be funny now, Cary thought, but he had also cleverly withheld his identity until she made a fool of herself. The charm and warmth of the cottage did not temper her irritation. Fixing him with a cold stare, she said, "There is no need to be rude."

When he did not respond, she moved into the kitchen. Gardener, handyman, or owner, she could just ignore him. She felt very much at home already in the cottage, and she could tolerate its owner. She ran her fingers over the counter tops, admiring the oak cabinets, noting the older but service-able appliances and the compact sink. With a table for two under the window, the cozy kitchen seemed a place to share intimacies. Various plastic and glass containers on the window ledge drew her attention. Chosen for their utilitarian rather than aesthetic value, they were sprouting attractively with greenery. Automatically Cary picked up a pot and sniffed.

"Hmm. Like chewing gum."

"Right. Spearmint," Spence said, pointing. "And that's applemint, and borage just starting. If you're not into herbs, you can replace them. But since you answered the ad, I thought you'd know herbs, maybe even be an herbalist?"

"I don't know one herb from another," Cary admitted. "In fact, I don't even know how to pronounce the word. I shift from 'erb to herb, never sure what's correct!"

"Most folks around here say herb, but you'll hear it

both ways." The friendly tone he'd used when he speaking of herbs again turned businesslike. He ticked off the usual formalities required when renting a place, pointing out the merits of the refrigerator, the mysteries of the stove, and the frailties of the water system. "We're on our own system here. Once in a while you may hear some clunking and gurgling if the pump acts up."

Uncomfortably aware of his closeness, Cary noticed how he deftly avoided any contact, even an inadvertent brush, with her. Clearly he preferred to maintain a certain aloofness, a distance between them. Leaning around her to open the kitchen door, he kept his arm above her head and waved with his right hand to check out the back area.

When Cary saw the backyard, she knew she would stay.

Several tall pines provided a cool canopy. A white wrought iron table with matching chairs shared a small bricked patio with a charcoal grill. It was a place to relax. Suddenly tired, she moved to the patio and slumped in a chair.

Her foot throbbed. She shifted one of the chairs to get more comfortable, thinking she had to walk back to see about her car, thinking of her long drive that day, and almost wishing she were back in the arms of her family in Barrymore.

She sighed deeply, but became alert again as the proprietor asked, "Something wrong?"

"No," she straightened. "No, I'm fine."

"I haven't been a very good host, have I? What you need is a cup of tea." He allowed a smile to touch the corners of his mouth. "I'll be right back." He turned toward the kitchen.

"Wait!" Cary was not about to let someone she'd just met start pampering her. "Don't bother. In a minute I'll see about my car."

"I'll take care of it. We can't have strangers thinking we're inhospitable 'way out here." He sauntered away.

Cary leaned back, letting the peacefulness wash over her. The walk from her car had taken its toll. Her foot had not yet regained its full strength after her back surgery a few months earlier. The nerve damage would take some months to repair itself. She tried to be patient, not one of her best traits, but often she became furious with her weakness. This was one of those times. Granted, the walk up the graveled road had not been planned; granted her little sports car might not be admirably suited for long drives. Still, she tried to keep her eyes open, not to be caught dozing.

Even as Cary's eyes closed, she found herself remembering Lanny raging in her parents' sitting room, accusing her of thinking the Randalls were "too good for a hardworking slob" from somewhere other than the grand old state of Virginia.

"You'll be back, Cary." Lanny's belligerence was not cushioned by the serenity of the room. "It's time you grew up. You've been under your daddy's and big brother's wing too long."

"Get out, Stockton!" Phillip had appeared suddenly in the doorway, his face furious.

"Lanny, we were never right for each other," Cary had protested wearily. "Please go."

"Get out," Phillip repeated. "We don't want another accident," and his voice held a sneer, "do we?"

"Phillip, we agreed it was an accident," Cary said, remembering all too vividly the angry shove from Lanny that had sent her reeling down the stairs. "An accident, just as Lanny and I were an accident, a relationship that shouldn't have happened."

"An accident! You came looking for somebody and you found me." Lanny's eyes glinted dangerously.

He had never apologized for what happened. If anything he had been angry when he sat beside her bed in the hospital. He must have realized that he was losing her, that whatever need had led Cary into his arms was gone. Her fall had simply punctuated the ending of their relationship.

Returning with tea, Spence looked at the resting girl, a woman in her mid twenties, brown hair neatly cut. He remembered the deep green of her eyes, those enticing long eyelashes. Pretty, yes. Maybe desirable. Okay, desirable. Well-dressed, well-spoken, yet curiously defensive. His impulse to examine her foot has been as natural as the impulse to stroke an animal that seemed hurt or wounded. And good business sense too, he reminded himself. Renting the cottage was purely a business matter. He needed the extra income. He didn't need somebody suing because she'd tripped in his thyme bed! He didn't need a female needing attention.

But the urge that caused him to pick her up and carry her across the field was simply that, a devilish urge to ruffle her feathers. Breathing evenly, her lips slightly parted, her dark hair trailing over one cheek, she might have been a college freshman rather than the administrative assistant that she'd announced rather shortly when he asked what she did. She looked pale and vulnerable, fragile, in her sleep.

Stop it, he told himself, you don't need another diversion; you don't need another woman. Defenseless she might seem now, but he knew the power of a woman to hurt, the cruelty lurking behind the sweetness. His lip curled as Darla's image taunted him, Darla loving, Darla promising, Darla caressing, Darla leaving. Spence tore his thoughts from Darla and her final deception and concentrated on the task at hand.

Cary started as the tea tray clanked against the iron table beside her. "Your tea, madame."

The tray contained two cups along with a pottery tea pot with bamboo handle, sugar and milk, and a plate heaped with brownies.

She started to protest, but his stern look and the wonderful aroma silenced her. "That smells wonderful!" she said. "It's certainly more than your ordinary tea bag."

"ThymeTable's special blend of mints, guaranteed to make you perk up and swear off ordinary tea forever."

She noted the pride in his voice, noted too that he tried to veil it. He stirred the teapot.

"Let it steep for a few minutes while you're resting."

Cary sat up even straighter and regarded her foot with something akin to anger.

"Called Johnny over at the Cove," Spence said. "He'll go down and check on your car." Just as he spoke, a solidly built young man with longish blond hair neatly tied in a ponytail rounded the corner. Spence called and waved to the boy who crossed the backyard to them.

"Hi, Johnny. This is Ms. Randall." Inwardly Cary approved of his use of the Ms. although she didn't want to start her sojourn here being extremely formal.

She held out her hand. "Call me Cary. Hello, Johnny."

The boy gave her an appraising look, apparently approved, and took her hand briefly.

"If you'll give him the keys, Johnny will go down and see about bringing your car up. Think it'll be a problem?" This last Spence directed to the youth.

"No problem. I checked it out as I came up. Some tricky driving and a push from Robert will do it."

Cary handed him the keys. "It's probably a little scratched up. I hit the bank when I slid off."

"Yeah, a few scratches." Johnny shrugged. "Nothing a new paint job won't cure."

"You're in luck," Spence said. "Johnny's cousin runs a paint and body shop in Asheville. He can take care of it."

There we go again, thought Cary. Everybody's determined to take care of me. "I'll see to it," she said ungraciously. "If you can just get it here for me."

Looking slightly hurt, Johnny jangled the car keys. "Back in no time." He grinned, and perhaps only half in jest asked, "Sure you trust me?"

Before Cary could mend her discourteous response, Spence waved Johnny away with a "See you, buddy." He poured the amber colored liquid into two mugs. "Help yourself to sugar or milk."

The tea was delicious. She savored both its taste and its aroma, and she bit into a brownie as if she hadn't eaten in hours. In fact, she hadn't eaten since her midmorning stop on the interstate for coffee and toast. She finished two brownies in record time while Spence's eyes remained fixed on the trees. He sipped his tea as if he were alone and quite content to be so.

Cary was caught up in the quietness as well, although her thoughts were as tumbled as the mass of clouds scuttling overhead. She was very much aware of the man at the table beside her. She remembered those sure fingers on her body, then mentally reproved herself, "that way disaster lies." She didn't want another man in her life, certainly not one both "ornery" and handsome. Why couldn't her landlord have been a kindly, elderly white-haired gentleman with a wife who baked apple pies and perhaps played the piano? Landlord. The term brought a smile unbidden to her lips.

"Some joke I don't know about?" Spence asked.

"I was thinking about the term 'landlord,'" Cary said. "Lord of the land. It must date from the Middle Ages and the feudal system."

"Yeah, when the landlord," Spence emphasized the word, "owned all that was on his estate, to do with it as he willed, work the men, protect the children, ravage the women and—"

"The good old days when men were men and women were . . . slaves," Cary interrupted.

Spence smiled but a cynical note crept into his voice. "The good old days, before banks and bankers."

"Bankers?" Cary said.

"Forget it. Anything else I can do to help you get settled in?" Spence said in his desk clerk voice.

"No. No thanks. I may go out for a few things."

Spence stood. "Come over later if you like, for a casserole and salad. No need to cook this first night."

Cary was certain that he was implying that she needed a rest and she didn't want to be adopted as a poor female needing attention. "There's no reason to feed me," she replied quickly, "unless you add meals to my rent."

"Ms. Randall, you're something else! We tend to be friendly around here. But play it your way." He turned to leave. "Here comes Johnny already with your car. Call if I can do anything else."

"Un, sorry, but I really need to be alone for awhile."

"It's your call and your cottage as long as you're timely with your rent." His eyes sparkled at his play on words. "But it was only dinner I was offering, something I'd do for any guest who arrives late or—in no shape to go for groceries."

She reddened and averted her eyes. She, so carefully molded into the Randall tradition of good manners was certainly at her worst today. Her landlord probably had other dinner guests, perhaps a wife or girlfriend. He surely was not cooking just for her. Dinner would give her a chance to relax and be more pleasant, redeem herself in her eyes, at least. "I, I'm sorry. Dinner would be great."

"Good. Just down the path and over through the field. To the big house you will go!" The last he semi-chanted in the tune reminiscent of the Thanksgiving song from childhood. He pointed toward the white farmhouse. "About seven."

With a nod, he went to meet Johnny. The boy leapt from the car as if he'd been driving MGs all his life. They conferred briefly, and with a final salute Spence strode toward his place.

"You can drive it just fine now." Johnny returned the car keys. "It's a just a little roughened up." Besides a few scratches and a slightly dented fender, he assured her, the MG needed no serious attention.

Within a few moments they agreed that Johnny would see to the car's repairs and set a time for a paint job. She laughed comfortably when he teased her about her driving style and skill.

Johnny jammed hands in jeans and slanted his head to the left, indicating his destination. "Gotta go. The Cove's calling. Robert helped with the car. Now I've gotta help with his water line."

Just what is this Cove and how far is it from here? Have I wandered into a commune or some cult back here in the mountains? And who is Robert? Cary wondered. She had a dozen questions she was on the brink of asking, but Johnny was gone before she could.

Chapter 2

Cary gave her lips just a touch of gloss and decided against any further attempt at doing her face. After all, this was hardly a real dinner date, just an invitation, simply an obligatory duty of the landlord. But she had showered long in the spacious bathroom and changed into a soft yellow flowing cotton skirt. She adorned the plain camp shirt with the one necklace she'd packed, a simple gold braid. The she put on low heels for the walk over to Spence's house.

Her stomach growled with hunger. Those brownies a few hours earlier had whetted her appetite. But the fluttery feeling in her stomach was more than hunger. It had been a long time since she'd had dinner with any man other than Lanny. And dinners with Lanny had not always been a pleasant experience. She remembered their "special night" at Riverside, marking their six months together. She'd been enthusiastically describing a newcomer to the college administration, a man who had impressed her with his quick grasp of institutional research.

Unmindful of Lanny's tightening lips, she had chatted about Tom Jones' first days at the office. "I kidded him about

his name. You know, Tom Jones the dashing hero . . ." She
had stopped, realizing that Lanny wouldn't recognize the
name of an eighteenth century novel and its hero. In an
instant Lanny had reached across the table and seized her
forearm harshly. In a voice violent enough to slice through
steel and cold enough to congeal her blood, he warned,
"Another word about this—," and his language turned vul-
gar, "and you'll be sorry you ever met him."

Lanny had risen slightly from his chair to grasp her arm.
Then he released it and sank back, glowering, and tossed
down the remainder of his wine. She had not bothered to
tell him that Tom was engaged, that she'd never spoken to
him outside the Administration building. For the next several days she wore long-sleeved blouses to hide the bruises
on her arm. It had been some time since she had been at
ease sitting opposite a man at dinner.

Cary admired the "character" of Spence's large two-story
frame house long before she arrived at the side entrance. It
had scrolled Victorian woodwork on the balcony and on the
widow's walk. The square widow's walk adorning the roof was
unusual in the mountains, having been an expected part of
houses on the coast where the sea captain's family could
climb to look out for the ship bringing the sailors home.
Perhaps the wife of the builder of this large rambling house
came from the coast or perhaps she simply wanted to assert
her individualism and decreed to her husband that, reasonable or not, she wanted a widow's walk. The house, newly
painted in white, was trimmed in green, the same green that
her cottage sported. It had a small side porch to which the
path had led her and a larger front porch complete with a
hanging swing and various pieces of green wicker furniture.
The uncluttered porch seemed to call out for bicycles,
children's toys, and various family paraphernalia. In its pristine state, it had the look of a bachelor's place. The side
porch looked more lived in. Work gloves were thrown on a

table which also held an assortment of buckets, a tennis racquet, and a few towels neatly stacked to the side.

She knocked and then stuck her head in the kitchen door at Spence's "Come in. I'm in the kitchen." Cary was not totally surprised that she was in fact the only guest, and she was not at all disappointed. At the counter, Spence sliced carrots for a fresh salad. The large, very well-equipped kitchen bespoke the presence of a man who apparently liked to cook or, mused Cary, was forced to cook for himself and spared little expense to do so efficiently.

"Dinner in fifteen minutes," Spence announced when Cary was seated on a cushioned church pew along one wall. "Would you like a glass of white wine first?" He was already taking a bottle from the refrigerator. "This is very local and very good, wins lots of prizes," he continued. "Biltmore Estate's winery."

From her vantage point she watched the final preparations. Her landlord moved easily and confidently about his domain. Cary approved the jaunty color scheme of bright yellow and bold blue gray. There wasn't a dark corner anywhere. Large pots of ivy and what must be herbs hung from beams and sat on counter tops, leaving plenty of room for various appliances.

The simple eggplant casserole was delicious, chunky and creamy. Spence seemed totally comfortable serving the green salad with his special dressing. "A concoction of ThymeTable's early herbs with a twist of this and a bit of that," he stated cagily as he noted the pleasure she took in the tasting.

"Some sweet little old lady's secret recipe?" Cary asked.

"That's a chauvinist remark if ever I heard one," Spence returned. "My secret recipe, just developed this afternoon. If you like it, it may be destined for greatness one day and be on the shelf next to Newman's. I'll give you the recipe."

Cary found herself relaxing in her landlord's presence.

They ate at an enameled table in the corner of the kitchen. A handwoven deep blue cloth covered the table, and soft cotton napkins matched the hue of the cloth. A spray of forsythia brightened the table. The dishes were pottery, somewhat heavy but splashed with an exuberant yellow that showed the hand of a happy potter or a slaphappy one. When she commented on the joyousness of the pattern, Spence explained, "One of the original group who moved here a few years back, Jon Dorsey, experimented with primary colors on the local clay. He became quite good. This is one of his earlier efforts, but I especially liked the colors. He gave me this set when he left the Cove."

He hesitated just slightly, then he went on, "These pieces always remind me of Jon. He was a free spirit with a total disregard for certain conventions."

"Such as?"

"Oh, such as marriage, such as taxes," Spence replied neutrally. "Jon's living happily in Mexico now. In fact, he's throwing pots on one hand and playing the stock market on the other. He's a good friend, but not one to settle down. I hear from him occasionally."

Cary forgot about Jon as she ate the casserole and buttered homemade rolls. She asked if Spence also numbered baking among his roles at the farm. Spence admitted, "No, I can't claim credit for the rolls. Mrs. Alison down the road bakes her 'raised rolls' a couple of times a week. She supplies her favorite men."

"And you supply?"

"I supply firewood in the winter and an occasional chore in the summer. Whatever she needs."

"Sounds fair enough," Cary said. "I'll have another, please."

Cary thoroughly enjoyed her food and she relaxed with her host. When his eyes lingered overly long on a tiny butter smudge on her upper lip Cary noticed and hastily dabbed at her lips.

The eggplant, Spence said, was one of his better dishes. "I wanted to impress you with my culinary skills," he said, "but you'll notice I didn't do much picking up around the house." As they were finishing the meal, Spence put tea on to steep. They carried their cups into the living room where piles of books were strewn around, a jacket tossed on a trunk, a pair of boots decorated the corner.

Spence swept a few books from the coffee table and placed the tea tray there. "Only more brownies for dessert," he offered.

"No, nothing else. The tea smells wonderful. I can see that my coffee habit is going to be replaced." Cary settled herself on the sofa and was grateful that Spence took the chair to her right. She could not ignore what this man's lithe good looks aroused in her. She was very much aware of his every move as he bent to settle the tray before her, as he leaned back totally at ease and crossed one leg over his knee. He, too, had changed, replacing jeans for trousers that did not mold to his body as had his jeans but spoke a casual grace. His shirt was not inexpensive; she sometimes bought the brand for her brother. Spence wore the shirt with the aplomb of a catalog model. Cary swallowed her tea and tried to think of anything but the maleness he exuded.

Spence said, "You're only my second tenant. I had Cary Randall pegged as ..uh, a little different."

Cary shifted her attention to his words and queried with her eyes.

"The lady who rented the cottage last summer was a genealogist from Maine. Thelma Brown. About sixty," his eyes twinkled, "with strictly sensible shoes and a vast family tree. She spent most of her time gone, in and out of cemeteries, digging among her roots, as she put it."

He didn't continue that the arrangement had suited

him fine. He didn't particularly want a young, pretty tenant.
He had tried to please with a home-cooked meal when what
he should do was escort her out of his living room immediately before he forgot what Darla had taught him so well.
Never trust a woman she'd reminded him as she drove away
in the car he was still paying for. He'd gone on with his life,
working harder, sleeping less, reading more, seething and
gritting his teeth every time he thought of her. And he did
think of her, Darla in his arms, absolutely his, so he had
thought, so he had thought.

Abruptly he asked, "And what will you do to occupy your
time here? The farm is somewhat isolated."

Spence's altered tone was not lost on Cary. How much
did she want to reveal to her host about her decision to leave
the job she liked, the family who protected her, the lover she
no longer even liked? She wasn't ready, she knew, to do more
than make casual after-dinner conversation.

"I'll do a lot of reading and some photography. Taking
pictures is a hobby of mine, one I want to work on. There's
never enough time around the edges of a full-time job." In
addition to her luggage, she'd packed her SLR camera, along
with a few accessories, lenses, and a tripod. She had entered
her black and white photos into a few local competitions at
her instructor's urging. He had praised her talents, her good
eye for composition but told her she needed to develop
greater patience. She had not taken any serious photographs
for over a year.

"Landscape? People? What do you concentrate on?"
asked Spence.

"I used to want to get great people pictures, but gradually I realized that my strong suit is not people," Cary con-
fessed. "What I do best is close ups, textures, woodgrain, old
buildings, farm machinery. I have worked mostly in black
and white, but with my close-up lens I can do wild flowers,
mushrooms, whatever."

For the next hour Cary's face grew animated and her eyes sparkled as she revealed her interest in capturing shadows, light, design. Spence fed her questions and showed a fair knowledge of cameras and a genuine interest in the topic.

"I want to try some close up work with a micro lens," Cary glance up. Spence's gaze had the intensity of a photographer analyzing every feature of his subject. She blushed and bit her lip in frustration, finishing the sentence, "and one of those reflective blankets."

Her prim-like posture had disappeared as she relaxed and she had tucked her legs under her on the sofa. Now she stood. Spence announced, "I'll walk you back to Rosemary."

Cary shook her head. "No need. I can follow the path."

She didn't want this evening to turn into a date and end with a man at her door. The waft of Spence's cologne brought a rush of yearning through her. What is this, she sternly reprimanded herself, I don't need and I don't want another man in my life. As Spence slipped into a jacket, she headed for the door.

"It was a wonderful meal, a wonderful evening . . ." she began.

"And it's not over yet," Spence finished. His slight touch at her elbow, nothing more than a gentleman's assistance, brought all her defenses to the fore.

"What do you mean?" Her glare directed at him was deflected since he was closing the door.

"I mean, purely and simply, dear tenant, that I am walking you home," Spence said dryly. "Don't get your hopes up. I haven't assaulted a woman in years. And I won't start now. Neither do I intend to get sued for carelessness if you fall and break your neck on my property!"

Cary was effectively silenced. Why should I even think he might try something? I'm getting paranoid, she told herself. Even as her thoughts were tumbling, the warm night's magic descended on her. On us? she wondered. They walked within the circle of his flash light within inches of each other, separated from the darkness. She muted her internal monologue and allowed the sounds of the evening to surround and enclose her. The country was certainly not as quiet as she had thought this afternoon. She could identify a far-off twinkly bell, a muffled lowing of a cow, the closer call of an owl.

And down the road, the shifting of gears as a truck started the upgrade. But what was that cacophony?

"Peepers," Spence said, quietly. "Lots of little announcers of spring. You'll get used to them."

He was right. They provided a backdrop of sound that was repetitive enough not to be bothersome.

"Here you are, safe at your door."

"Darn." Cary stumbled slightly as a pebble shifted under her foot. Spence swung the flashlight to the door and she mis-stepped. Right against his body.

Even as he caught her in his proverbially waiting arms, Cary stiffened warily. But for a long moment she savored the comfort of resting her chin against his chest, of breathing against the hair at his open collar. Twice in one day she'd been pressed against his chest. He held her firmly. She heard his heart's rhythm thudding even as it seemed her own had stopped. A small sigh escaped Cary even as she willed herself to disengage her body from his nearness. She knew if she remained another moment, her vulnerability would be too apparent. Tenderness was something she could not deal with now.

Recognizing the quickening of his breath and the hardness of his body, Cary pulled herself from his arms.

"Are you . . . ?" Spence started.

"Are you . . ." Cary said at the same moment.

He stepped back from the impact of the anger in her voice and eyes. He didn't finish his "are you okay?" as Cary went on, "satisfied now?"

"Satisfied?" Spence returned. "Hardly. But then I wasn't looking for satisfaction. Is this some kind of duel we're having and I don't know the rules?"

Cary didn't meet his eyes, realizing again that she had assumed an attitude on Spence's part, but unwilling to admit it.

"Don't give me that hurt little girl look. When I want to be satisfied," Spence deliberately underlined the word with his sarcasm, "I'll look elsewhere. Now I've done the landlordly thing and seen you to your door. I'll leave you to any interpretation you like for your falling into my arms!"

He walked away. Not even in a huff, she thought ruefully. She wanted to call out her thanks to be polite if nothing else, but she slammed the door instead. She didn't notice the circle of light pause as Spence looked back briefly.

Spence shrugged. Yes, for a moment there he had wanted Cary fiercely, physically. Maybe he even wanted her to ask him in. But he knew that if she had, he would have said no, thank you no. Since Darla had left him months ago, Spence had determined not to trust any woman again as he had her, the sensual, the sexy, the, Spence smiled grimly, the snake. At thirty-two, Spence had not realized how vulnerable he was to Darla. And she had used his love and his trust to almost ruin him financially. And she had ruined him, he thought, for another woman. When he remembered her silky long blond hair, her curvaceous body, her absolute giving of herself (again, so he had thought), he had no trouble disregarding the occasional flirtatious smile, the sometimes openly inviting glances of women he hardly knew.

Cary's closeness had brought the first flame of more than passing interest. She had felt good for that instant in his arms. Her brazen assumption that he, or he supposed, any man was on the verge of attacking and devouring her with or without her consent had dampened his ardor. He told himself as he returned to his sofa that he and Cary would get along just fine, going their separate ways.

The next morning, Cary awakened refreshed, lolled for long minutes in the shaft of sunlight that the lightly pulled curtains allowed to warm her bed. "Busy old sun, unruly fool," she murmured aloud; her poetry quoting had irritated Lenny, but she'd never conquered the habit. It had gone underground, escaping only as a hardly audible word or two.

She grinned. Here she could quote to herself as much as she pleased. She stretched, remembering John Donne's poem celebrating the glories of the two lovers and their pleasure of the night. "Busy old sun," she jumped up and swept the curtains wide, "you'll find no lovers here."

As she pulled on her jeans, she thought of Spence and his abrupt leave-taking. "Nope, no lovers here."

In a few minutes she went to explore the kitchen. Soon she was sipping a strong hot tea with honey and toasting a dark sweet bread she'd found in the freezer compartment of the refrigerator. Aside from a variety of jars and tins of herbs, the pantry was bare. She'd enjoy a trip to the grocery store where, she told herself, she'd buy all her favorite things without regard for calories or fat grams.

It was almost noon when the telephone rang.

"Good God, Cary, where in the hell are you?" Phillip rarely bothered with a civil hello, especially when he disapproved of whatever she was doing.

"I'm drying my hair in the sunshine and seducing three or four of the locals." Cary couldn't help it.

Phillip responded as she expected, not noticing her wry tone. "You're worrying our parents, being totally irresponsible."

"Phil, please." Cary took a deep breath. "I knew Mother would want to take over if I stayed. She doesn't think I can be trusted to stay safe and healthy in my apartment. I would have called later today. In fact, I'll call Mother when we hang up. How did you get this number?"

"Went through your desk at work and found a couple of ads for rentals. Now, just what . . . ?"

Cary interrupted. "Phillip, I am here. I am fine. I won't be home or back to work for awhile."

"The parents . . ."

"You haven't seen Lanny, have you?"

"That SOB. He came yelling over to my office, acting like you'd hurt him!" A small note of satisfaction entered Phillip's voice. "He won't be back."

"Good-by, Phillip. I'll call." Cary went back to the kitchen. Unable to relax and in a frenzy of having to do something, she busied herself washing all the dishes and utensils in the kitchen, none of which really needed the thorough scrubbing she gave them. Totally immersed in her self-inflicted chores, Cary gave a start when Spence's shadow suddenly darkened the door.

His unannounced presence caught her off guard and sent her senses tingling. In a flash, she was less than welcoming. "Checking up on me like a good landlord should?"

"What is it with you, Ms. Randall?" What might have started as a simple pleasantry on Spence's part shifted at her abrupt question and his voice was cool. He wore a lightweight suit, looking every bit the smart executive but there was an air of grimness about him.

Cary dried her hands. While he looked as if he belonged in an office, she must look like a representative of the local cleaning society. Spence did not step over the doorway, and in her agitation she did not think to invite him in.

"I came by to see if the cottage needed anything, any supplies, any light bulbs that don't work?" He leaned on the doorframe. "And to say I'll be gone for a few days."

"Business?" A silly question and not her concern.

"Business," he repeated and did not elaborate.

"Johnny can take care of any emergencies that come up. Or Mary, his mother. I told her to see to your every need."

"I don't need anything."

"Maybe, maybe not, Ms. Cinderella," Spence announced, a glimmer of a smile almost erasing the grimness. "But at the rate you're going, perhaps I should bring back a supply of dishwashing detergent."

Cary eyed all the suds in the sink and grinned back. "Or better yet, a batch of romance novels. I'm here to relax after all. Appearances to the contrary, I am not a kitchen maid."

"You're cute when you grin, Cary, you should try it more often." Spence turned and with a slight wave was gone.

Cary felt a curious loss, a vacancy as she heard his car crunch off. Obviously this herb farmer had business to transact. Or, her heart gave a tiny lurch, or he had a girlfriend waiting for him. In their long talk after dinner, he had not mentioned any involvement, but she doubted he lived the life of a monk. However, she had done most of the talking and had not attempted to pry into his love life.

Suddenly she was intensely curious about the cottage. Had Spence chosen the furniture, the curtains, the very dishes she was rinsing? Who had decided on the well-framed hummingbird art prints and the cushions that so perfectly complemented the sofa's fabric? Cary shook her head to clear it of the strangely unwelcome thought of a woman in Rosemary Cottage, a woman in Spence's life.

The next day, Cary was lying under the towering evergreen, a glass of iced coffee on the ground beside her lounge. She breathed deeply and felt the peacefulness descend on her as naturally as the dew fell on the fields around her while she slept. A book on photography lay unopened on her lap. She had strolled through the fields, up the gravel road, alongside the fenced pastures further up the mountain, not yet ready to trust those large grazing cows that regarded her with a passive curiosity. She paid attention to the shapes of fallen

oaks and pines, to the texture of roughened barns and leaning outbuildings, to the clumps of moss and early flowers,
boulders and fence posts. She had not yet taken her camera.
First, she wanted to "see" without looking through its lenses.

Even as she read, walked, and became comfortable in
Rosemary Cottage, she had been resolute in refusing to think
of grim-faced Spence—every time she caught herself thinking! And that had been often. ThymeTable Farm and its owner
had begun to intrigue her.

Cary jumped up with anticipation. Today she was going
to walk over to the Cove, half a mile or so through the fields,
the collection of buildings still occupied by some of the
people who had established themselves there several years
earlier in an informal kind of communal organization. When
Johnny stopped to drive her car into town, he'd told her his
mother expected her anytime.

In the midmorning light, the farm was as peaceful a place
as she could imagine. "And I was green and happy there,"
she quoted one of her favorite poets softly, looking around
her.

Walking over to visit Johnny's mother, Cary admired the
various beds of herbs. Granted that she recognized very few,
she admired the well-tended gardens, stopping to pinch
and smell more closely. Sage was one of the few she was sure
of. She remembered her grandmother telling her as she
stuffed the Thanksgiving turkey, that sage was supposed to
contribute to longevity and that it had been used as a hot
drink long before tea became popular. The sage bed was
fairly large and the sage was almost a foot high, its leaves
pebbly to the touch. Cary skirted another section of plantings
which she didn't recognize and made a mental note to ask
Mary about the different herbs. This morning she felt good.
The sky was blue, the air crisp, with a radiant purity.

A woman of indeterminate age, maybe forty, maybe fifty,
stepped from the larger cabin. Her long hair, once blond,

now had some streaks of gray showing. It was restrained in a loosely braided single plait that reached almost to her waist. Her faded jeans and tee shirt revealed a thin frame. Her face was open, slightly freckled, free of makeup, and friendly.

"Hi, I'm Johnny's mother, Mary. And I know you're Spence's new boarder." Her voice was soft and measured. She held out her hand to Cary.

"It's beautiful here. Already I feel as if I could stay forever," Cary grasped Mary's firm hand.

Mary acknowledged the comment with a tilt of her head.

"Come in and have some tea. I'm just taking a break from my job."

"I've just had coffee, but tea sounds wonderful! I think I'm an addict already."

The room surprised Cary. She supposed she'd expected a certain rustic look; instead she found a combination of living room and office. A computer complete with scanner, copier, and fax machine sat on a table surrounded by book-cases overflowing with books, magazines, and various pieces of pottery. Mary quickly cleared the screen and with a few taps exited the program.

Cary looked puzzled and Mary motioned her to a comfortable chair and laughed, "Yes, I do work."

"Here?"

"Technical translating and some editing. My speciality is French and German to English, mostly for very specialized journals." She pointed to several technical journals lying about. When Mary went to the kitchen, Cary paid more attention to the room. It had a careless, lived-in look: boots left near the door, cushions on the sofa and floor, a quilt draped over the easy chair; the walls held grapevine wreaths, oil land-scapes, a well-marked calendar and a variety of framed and unframed photographs. Light flooded the room through deep-set, curtainless windows.

Cary listened with interest as Mary described some of

her clients and her work. But this visit was a perfect time to add to her limited knowledge of her landlord. She asked about ThymeTable Farm with what she hoped was a casual air. Mary answered tersely that Spence bought the farm almost three years ago when an old friend was unable to continue his efforts to create his life-long dream of being totally self-sufficient.

"Dan Abbott wrote for back-to-the-earth magazines. Dan sold Spence the farm, took off to live his dream in Alaska, and then died in a few months." Mary sipped her tea reflectively.

"Spence hasn't tried for total self-sufficiency, but he intends to make ThymeTable a financial success. Being a success is probably in his blood." Intrigued, especially about that ambiguous comment, Cary didn't want to seem too curious, so she changed the subject.

"Doesn't it get lonely here? I know Asheville's an easy drive, but there aren't many people close by." Cary mentally compared the density of the population with her apartment building with its constant sense of movement as college students, singles, and young families hurried in and out.

"I guess we are reclusive by nature—and by choice. For the time being, Spence doesn't need a lot of people. And he had Darla." Mary stopped abruptly.

"Darla?"

"Bring your cup and let's go outside. I'll show you around." Obviously Mary intended to say nothing more about Darla or Spence.

"Johnny has fixed up a couple of rooms above the apple house." Mary pointed to a two- story structure, built partly into the bank. The lower portion was of stone, and steps led to a tiny landing at the upper story. "He shares the kitchen in the house with me, but he decided a few months ago to move out. He needs his space, he tells me."

Mary shrugged indulgently. "Now that he's got a steady

girlfriend he doesn't want to entertain her in my living room, especially since I'm likely to be working at my computer."

Mary pointed out the barn and a building for equipment storage. While the place seemed fairly well kept, it was also noticeable that more work could be done. She went on talking about Johnny.

"I know Johnny will want to get married. He's always said he'd never be like his father, but Suzanne's going to college this fall. So I hope they'll wait."

"Doesn't he want to go to college?"

"He's into cars. This year of working with his cousin has made him more interested. He's been to the community college to see about the automotive program, may be going to night school and working at the garage during the day."

She picked up a couple of rakes and stood them inside the barn. "I love the country but my expertise has never been outside work." Mary sighed. "When we moved here, we thought living in the country would be a lot simpler than it is."

Cary learned that the original group who purchased the surrounding land had moved to the western part of North Carolina for a variety of reasons. Mary wanted to escape the drug scene in Chicago where she'd worried about Johnny. The others simply wanted to get away from their urban environments. Gradually the younger owners moved away, selling to the six of the original group who remained. That explained the empty structures. Mary and Johnny stayed along with Robert, an introvert "without equal" according to Mary, and his son. Two sisters who had taken early retirement from big city school systems also remained.

"Everybody's gone into town now, so I'll introduce you the next time you come over. Robert is in his early sixties and not doing too well right now. He operates a rare book finding service on a limited basis from his home. Justin, that's his son, visits him as often as his new medical practice allows.

Alice and Agnes taught English and math for their required quota of years, as they put it, and they do some volunteer work in town and tend a small garden and enjoy their goats. They pretty much do their own thing. We all do. We share the expenses, still get along well enough to share the mortgage although we now have a workable legal agreement," Mary explained. "We don't want to think about having to reconsider our options and either sell out or fix up the place. I'm in no hurry to move on. My fax machine keeps the work coming in."

Cary found Mary, like her son, easy to talk to and soon she was telling her about her family.

"Dad's an investment broker, has a good business and does a lot of financing of developments. Mom has never worked except," Cary summarized, "for running just about every club she's ever been in and doing loads of volunteering."

She went on, "Phillip's my brother, my only and older brother, my boss-brother. He's always tried to boss me, and now he's married to the perfect lady, who dominates him." Cary underlined the words. "Alecia actually makes a lot of Phillip's decisions, but he doesn't know it. Or maybe he does and that's why he watches over me and tries to keep me straight!"

"I can't imagine you need to be straightened out," Mary said, looking appraisingly at the clean-cut girl.

"Well," Cary said, "Phillip has already called and given me what for because I left home so suddenly."

Mary snapped a twig and asked, "Suddenly?"

"I disappointed him, and maybe my parents, that's for sure." She turned aside so Mary wouldn't see the wave of despair that swept over her. "And here I am . . . . on indefinite leave from my job and my family." She hoped Mary didn't hear the unspoken "and someone else."

They wandered somewhat aimlessly around the grounds

and stopped to lean on the wooden fence. Mary tactfully asked, "What kind of work did you do?"

Cary told her of her work at the local college, work that had fallen easily into her lap when she graduated from college with a degree in history, a minor in English, and no definite plans. The dean was an old family friend. He had talked her into taking the temporary position until Mrs. Adolphos returned from maternity leave. Her leave, however, included following her husband to his native Greece.

Cary had stayed on, at first intrigued with the intricacies of college politics (from her new perspective of non-student). Cary described her job, her several bosses, her playing on the staff volleyball team, but she stopped short of revealing her involvement with Lanny. How could she explain her involvement with the thirty-year-old, dark, aggressive, new owner of the refurbished and renamed Lanny's Grill? When Mary realized that Cary was avoiding the subject of men, they discussed students and languages. Cary practiced her "small French and less Spanish." The afternoon passed easily and quickly.

"I don't know an herb from a spice," Cary admitted as she thanked Mary for a lovely visit, "but surrounded by all these odors and planting beds I'm really interested. I'd like to know more."

Mary gave her a long look. "The Grayson sisters can help you if you're serious. So can we. We've picked up quite a bit of knowledge just being around and helping out in busy times. Will you be here a few days," she asked, "or weeks?"

"I'm not sure yet. I just . . . have to see."

"Spence will be back tonight or in the morning," Mary volunteered.

"Tomorrow I'm taking my camera out on a safari of sorts," Cary said. "I can't laze around day after day, just waiting . . ."

"Not waiting for Spence?"

"Hardly," Cary said. It was only a small fib. Although she

knew she might not be waiting, she certainly anticipated seeing him. Without being elbow-deep in dish water.

"Ah, that's wise. Who knows?" Mary said. "Spence is likely to dash off at any time."

"Dash off?"

"Spence swears he joined the Peace Corps to escape the charms of his college girlfriend," Mary said with a shrug. "I'd say he had purer motivation but his years in Senegal did keep him out of her clutches. Then, at least."

"Are you trying to tell me something, Mary? He won't have to dash off anywhere to escape from me."

At Mary's noncommital glance, Cary declared, "I just met the man this week! I've had one dinner and one . . . . well," she laughed, "several brownies with him and that's all."

"You didn't know him before you got here?"

"Of course not. I saw an ad for a cottage and here I am. No ulterior motives."

"Good. 'Cause Spence is a good friend. And he's vulnerable right now."

"Because of Darla?"

Mary nodded shortly. "Want me to drive you back to Rosemary? I'm going into the post office."

"Thanks but no. I'm not an invalid. And my landlord is safe from me."

On the walk back Cary found herself wondering: just what is the difference between an herb and a spice? She'd have to look it up. But semantics aside, she was curious about Spence and Darla. Of course, he'd have a girlfriend.

Probably he was with her at the very moment. By the time she entered her cottage and put her foot on the footstool, she had convinced herself that the next time she saw Spence he'd have Darla on his arm.

She found in the dictionary that an "herb" was any plant used as a medicine or seasoning and that an herb's stem withers away after each season's growth. "Mint, thyme, basil, and sage are herbs," she read. Spices, on the other hand, are "vegetable substances used for seasoning." They add flavor and aroma. Pepper, cloves, nutmeg, and cinnamon were given as examples. I'm glad to know that I'm definitely on an herb farm, Cary mused, since I haven't seen or smelled any cinnamon trees. She picked up the book on herbs and tried to read; she flipped on the television and then turned it off. She rearranged the cushions and magazines. After checking her camera and getting her gear together, she made herself a sandwich. I should have asked Mary to tell me more about Darla she thought. Why, I don't even know if Spence was married to her or is separated or divorced. She had noticed that he wore no wedding ring, but then, lots of men didn't.

Unable to concentrate as twilight descended, Cary dusted each room. Then she read all about rosemary; around eight o'clock she decided to mop the kitchen floor.

When she heard a light tap and looked up, flushed and damp from fighting with the wring mop, Spence grinned at her through the pane. He opened the door and exclaimed, "Ms. Cinderella, I presume? I leave you up to your elbows in dish water and return to find you scrubbing an immaculate floor."

"Oh!" sputtered Cary, her heart instantly on fast time. "And just where is Darla?"

If Spence's sudden appearance surprised Cary, her defiant question apparently astonished him. The good humor drained from his face as if she'd struck him. They stood in absolute silence. Cary wanted to apologize. What had come over her? She'd been scrubbing, perhaps unconsciously trying to eradicate any thoughts of Spence and Darla, and the words had rashly sprung out of her mouth.

Spence simply stood, the sparkle gone from his eyes, his jaw set. He held the door wide and she knew he'd slam it as he left. He assumed a theatrical smirk. "Frankly, my dear tenant, where Darla is is none of your business."

Chapter 3

After Spence left her standing like some sudsy princess marooned in a flood of embarrassment, Cary astonished herself by bursting into laughter. She must strike him as both naive and silly. That's the best she could hope for. She only hoped he didn't think she was jealous! She collapsed on the newly mopped floor in what her mother called "a fit of giggles." Finally she put away the cleaning materials, set out her hiking boots, methodically checked her camera and lenses, and mentally ticked off some of the more photogenic possibilities she'd seen around ThymeTable.

Decidedly lighthearted at her resolution to stop thinking about the mysteriously elusive Darla and the apparently snared Spence, she went to bed and slept soundly.

The next morning Cary had her coffee before the sun rose. She was determined to do her own thing and put her landlord in his own place—somewhere other than her mind.

She slung her light knapsack with her camera gear over her shoulder and picked up a stout walking stick. She didn't want to risk stepping on a snake, poisonous or not, so she intended to create sufficient movement to warn any slithering creature of her whereabouts. She surveyed the early morning scene.

"Up, up my friend and quit your books or surely you'll grow double. Up, up." She shifted to another Wordsworth poem. "Come forth into the light of things. Let nature be your teacher."

"Speaking of light," she mused aloud. And minutes later she settled herself to catch the first rays of the sun through the cobwebby cracks of the gray barn beyond Mary and Johnny's place. For the next hour Cary trudged, stooped, clicked, totally immersed in the glory of the morning. Her efforts today would be more practice than perfect, but she remembered her instructor's admonitions: "Never be satisfied with one angle. Keep moving, keep moving," and again, "Wait for the light."

Cary stopped to introduce herself to Alice and Agnes Grayson who were working in their barn. From the Mid-west and in their early eighties, they announced that neither had ever married.

"Agnes' beau died in the war," Alice said.

"And Alice refused two perfectly nice boys because one wanted her to live on a farm and the other lived with his parents and intended to stay there!" Agnes said.

"I was young," conceded Alice, "and couldn't see me on a farm then."

"And look at you now. You're like two petite earth mothers!" teased Cary. Both ladies had perfect posture and a certain regal air, but at the moment they were in men's overalls, plaid shirts, and sturdy work boots. Although neither weighed more than a hundred pounds, they tossed pitchforks of hay easily.

Cary snapped picture after picture of the goats and their antics as they pranced and nudged their owners.

"They're Nubians mostly, the same kind that Carl Sandburg raised, or his wife did, on their farm outside

Hendersonville, and this doe's a La Mancha," Alice told her proudly.

"I've read about the Sandburg farm, Connemara," Cary interjected. "Doesn't the National Park Service run it now?"

The sisters nodded and proudly surveyed their goats. "We sell the milk to a couple of families whose children are allergic to cow's milk, and we have to let the babies go now and then." Agnes went on. "We can only manage ten to fifteen. And they do take some caring for."

"Spence and Robert help during the winter, and Mary and Johnny are indispensable." Alice fed a carrot to a greedy goat. "We do love it here at the Cove."

Cary wondered if she imagined the wistfulness in her tone, the unspoken edge of worry.

"Let me help while I'm here," she impulsively offered. "I'll add goat lore to everything else I'm learning here. I mean it. I'll get these prints developed right away. Goats are natural posers, especially Brutus and Angela."

"We're naturally curious—" began Alice, timidly.

"Ninety-nine point nine percent of the time," interrupted Agnes.

"About how long you'll be staying at Rosemary," finished Alice. "It's good to have a nice young person nearby." Cary heard the emphasis on "nice" and immediately her thoughts ran to Darla.

"I'm curious too, to see how long I stay," she said truthfully.

"And I'm also curious—one hundred percent curious—about," she hesitated. Her mother would have frowned at such outright nosiness.

"What, dearie?"

"Mary mentioned the name of Darla, and I wondered, I wondered about her and Spence." Cary blushed like a fourteen-year-old. "I know it's none of my business."

The sisters exchanged glances, and Alice raked at some

loose hay. "We really don't know. Spence keeps his personal life to himself."

Cary started to apologize for her curiosity, but Alice went on, "She came in a flurry and she left in a flurry."

"And in between she flounced around as if she owned the place or soon would." Agnes clamped her mouth shut. "And that's all we know."

"Come into the house, Cary, and taste some of our goat cheese. We learned to make it after we moved here, from Dan Abbott. We're proud of it."

"Just a quick taste, then."

"Sister," admonished Agnes when Alice bent over with coughing. "It's time for your medicine."

In their cottage, Alice took a jar from the cupboard and poured out two or three spoonfuls. At Cary's quizzical look, Agnes explained, "It's our home remedy for coughs. We call it Agnes-mony, because I concocted it from a recipe I found in a book on herbal cure."

"What's in it?"

"Dried parsley and dried agrimony flowers and boiling water. Of course, we let them steep and cool and then we strain it. Simple and effective. At least for our early spring coughs."

Cary shook her head. "I'm learning more than I ever expected to."

She ate goat's cheese with a slab of Mrs. Alison's fresh bread, declared everything delicious, and promised to return for a visit soon.

"Don't be alarmed if you see me out early taking pictures when the light is good," she said.

"You'd have to get up very early, Cary, to beat these old bones out of bed! Stop by anytime!"

Cary twirled her walking stick as she strolled back to Rosemary in high spirits. She had lain in the early dew to snap closeups of some strange looking waxy plants; she had knelt to check out misted moss on fence posts, and she'd waded through a small stream to photograph a swirl of water. Her boots were muddy, her knees were muddy, her elbows were muddy, and her face was smudged.

After she'd snapped several pictures of ancient tin signs celebrating the merits of root beer and Martha White flour and Lucky Strike cigarettes, she'd gone inside one of the sheds to try to capture the dust particles themselves caught in the shafts of sunlight. Her hair held straw and a sprinkling of dust.

"Oh no," Cary groaned, melodramatically throwing her hand to her forehead. She recognized the late model American car in front of Rosemary. Newly washed, of course. Her brother wouldn't drive a car that wasn't as clean as the carwash could make it. He'd likely made a carwash stop in Asheville.

"The door wasn't locked," Phillip stated pointedly, "so we let ourselves in."

"Hello Phillip, Alecia," Cary said, tugging at her boots. She left them at the back door and shrugged carefully out of her knapsack. She held up her hands.

"Excuse me while I wash up. I didn't expect company."

"Obviously," Phillip said.

Alecia, in a tailored suit and pumps, adjusted her necklace, and picked up smoothly, "We should have called first, but Phillip wanted to surprise you."

"What in God's name have you been doing, Cary? Auditioning for some mud wrestling contest? The mud won."

"I might ask you the same question, Phillip." Cary ignored his attempt at humor. "What are you doing here?"

"Came to see you, to see how you're doing," he replied. "Came to see if you need anything, money, advice."

"Moral support," Alecia added.

Cary gritted her teeth in frustration. But she didn't want to appear ungracious about their visit. Her brother had always "looked after her interests" as he put it, "looked over her shoulder" as she put it.

"Phillip," she admonished gently, "I had a job, remember. I don't need money. I don't, in fact, need anything. Except," and although she smiled her tone was firm, "for some privacy and the chance to think things through."

"Honey," Alecia said, "we don't want to intrude on your precious privacy, but Phillip was naturally concerned when you left." She glanced at Cary's foot, and went on before Cary could reply, "We're staying in the area for a few days and have checked in at the Radisson. We're always looking for property, and certainly there's still undeveloped land around here."

"Phillip, did you come land looking as an excuse to keep me under surveillance?" Cary exploded. "I am not some child!"

Phillip appeared unperturbed by her outburst. He leaned back on the sofa. "We wanted to be sure you're okay."

Alecia smiled, "And to tell you that Lanny intends to sell the grill. Good riddance." With a wave of her hand, Alecia dismissed Lanny. "But Smith is in New York, enjoying the Big Apple. Rumor has it that a certain heiress to most of upstate New York is also there."

Cary laughed. "I've been out of Barrymore for less than a week and the rumor mill is grinding!"

"Smith didn't linger, dear," Alecia chimed in, "to suffer the pangs of unrequited love."

Their families had tried to pair up Cary and Smith for years with the two of them smiling but uninterested. Cary thought Smith was good-looking but bland, and he thought of Cary as a cousin. Occasionally, under family pressure, they had attended public functions together.

Cary made coffee and took the tray into her waiting guests. "This is our first real trip to the western part of North

Carolina," Alecia picked up the conversation smoothly. "It's absolutely gorgeous. But that road up here!"

Cary wasn't about to tell them that she'd started her stay here with her car in the ditch. They discussed the region, the weather, their parents, all carefully avoiding any further mention of Cary's personal life. She agreed to join them for dinner at Asheville's world-class hotel, the Grove Park Inn.

"Meet us in our hotel lobby around seven-thirty," Phillip said, "and we can go in one car." He surveyed Cary's mud-caked clothes. "You do have a dress?"

"Oh, I'll find something. You'll just have to make do with whatever I can throw together!"

Alecia looked a trifle disconcerted and Cary went on, "I didn't pack much. This is a farm, you know. I didn't expect to be dining elegantly. But I'll not disgrace you."

She showed them to the door. "See you later and I promise to be cleaner."

There was no evidence of Spence and Cary found herself thinking of him too often. It was his face that swam before her eyes as she took a brief late afternoon nap, his face that kept interrupting her concentration on the book on herbs, his face with that devilish twinkle that had her singing as she showered, "I'm gonna wash that man right out of my hair, right out of my hair, right out of my hair."

As she prepared to leave, Johnny's truck pulled into her driveway. Mary hopped out, a covered plate in her hands.

"Hi. Hey, don't you look great! Do you have a date or do you always wear silk for dinner? You don't have to answer that nosy question. That green is lovely, and," she sniffed, "is that Diamonds perfume? I recognize it anywhere." She extended the plate.

"Thanks, Mary, for the compliment and thanks for . . ." Cary bent to smell the covered dish.

"Mrs. Alison sent you her special buttermilk pie, as a welcome to the neighborhood."

Johnny stuck his head out the truck window. "She gave us its twin. She always bakes in batches, never just one thing at a time."

Cary gave her skirt a swirl, careful of the still warm pie. "Do I look okay for the Grove Park Inn? I've only seen articles and advertisements about it, and I don't want to disgrace my 'date.'"

Before she could explain that her date was her brother and sister-in-law, Johnny revved the engine and yelled, "Come on, MaryMom, I've got to get you home and pick up Suzanne. Rush it."

Mary said, "You'll do your date proud. See you." She hurried into the truck and with a great grinding of gears, Johnny roared off.

Oh, well, Cary thought, she won't have to worry that Spence is in any danger from me. As Cary stopped her car at the end of her drive, a battered yellow Volvo went by. She saw just a flash of very blond hair and very handsome face. The driver threw up his hand as if he knew her. Someone out enjoying the country or someone lost, she thought, as she pulled onto the graveled road.

The Grove Park Inn, which opened in the summer of 1913, was the dream of E.W. Grove of Bromo-Quinine and Grove's Tasteless Chill Tonic fame, and decades later, enlarged and modernized, it certainly lived up to its reputation for charm and elegance. The dinner was splendid.

Phillip indulged in the hot seared Whiskey Salmon and Alecia nibbled at her broiled turkey breast with its tangy fruit chutney. Cary devoured every bite of the Spinach Tortellini Blue Ridge with smoked Gouda cheese sauce. Both Phillip and Alecia were enchanted by the service and the ambiance.

Cary felt outshone by Alecia in her lovely backless black outfit. Alecia had a flare for elegant dressing and Phillip encouraged her. The evening was off to a good start when

Cary quoted Byron's lines to her sister-in-law: "She walks in beauty like the night of cloudless climes and starry skies."

"Glad to see you looking so . . ." Phillip said.

"So tidy," Cary teased him.

"Quite. And I'm delighted to escort both of you."

"No suitable escort for you yet, out here in the wilds, Cary?" Alecia asked. Her eyes roamed over the well-dressed men in the lobby where they were having drinks before dinner. "Although this is hardly the wilds. Very civilized."

"I don't work as rapidly as you do in the men department," Cary returned, "And I'm hardly panting for a man at this point."

Even as she declared her disinterest, Cary blushed. Spence's image flashed before her, his bare chest, his strong arms, and his grim face.

Alecia raised her eyebrows, but said nothing.

Cary realized somewhere between her tortellini and coffee that the conversation returned several times to land values, to zoning regulations, to housing development opportunities in the western part of the state. When Phillip was discoursing on a golf course and condominium complex some twenty miles away, a light dawned.

"Phillip, you're not here because of me!" she exclaimed. "You're into some business venture, aren't you? What happened to that development on the lower coast? That was supposed to occupy your time and money, the family money for the next few years?"

Phillip's left eyelid twitched slightly, the only sign of discomfort as he sipped his coffee appreciatively. "The coastal thing is okay for now," he said. At a glance from his wife, he amended, "Okay, but there have been some difficulties with the local zoning commission and all the publicity about the coastal environmentalists trying to save this and save that hasn't helped. Sales are slow right now."

When Phillip admitted to slow sales, he meant practically

non-existent. So what was Phillip doing hundreds of miles from his investment with all his talk of local regulations?

"This Inn was constructed in less than twelve months," Alecia changed the subject by reading from the menu. "It must have taken thousands of workers! Think of the Suntip project and how long that took, even with modern construction equipment."

"Phillip, your company's not in trouble, is it?" Cary ignored the attempted diversion.

"No trouble that I can't handle." He beckoned a nearby waiter.

"No trouble at all," Alecia stated. "Now, shall we have dessert?" Alecia could eat dessert four times a day and still keep her body the envy of all her friends. Sometimes, Cary was willing to bet, she did eat dessert four times a day just to annoy those same less-svelte friends.

"Yes, dear, let's celebrate Cary's new-found freedom from the constraints of work and, er, love with something gooey and chocolately."

"And rich!" finished Alecia. Alecia loved the word "rich" whether it related to men or food.

Cary resisted dessert in favor of a frothy cappuccino. As they left their table and made their way through the maze of diners, Cary heard, "The red MG lady!" The speaker was young, blond, good-looking, and impeccably dressed in blue blazer and perfectly creased trousers of a soft, creamy fabric. He pushed his chair back, with an apologetic nod to the older couple at his table, and put out his hand.

"Hi, let me introduce myself. I'm Justin Moreland," he said, and when Cary smiled in bewilderment, he continued, "I know you're staying at ThymeTable. You haven't met my dad yet, but he lives in the Cove. Robert Moreland."

"Oh," stuttered Cary, "Hi. You passed me as I was coming out of Rosemary. I recognize your hair!"

Alecia eyed the young man with her usual predatory look.

Alecia often looked at handsome males with an intensity that left them confused when she never followed through. Phillip too was waiting.

"I'm Cary Randall. And this is my brother Phillip and his wife Alecia." Aware that they were cluttering up the passageway, Cary hurried on, "We must get on. I have the drive back, and already . . . "

"I heard you ditched the MG once already," Justin grinned. "I'll be on the lookout as I return. While I'm here, perhaps we can get together, come into the big city together!"

"Perhaps," said Cary, "but I'm a little more cautious about men than about my driving." "Mary can vouch for my honor," said Justin. "Seriously, I'd like you to meet Dad. Maybe dinner one evening."

"I'd like that." Belatedly aware that Justin still held her hand, Cary withdrew it and nodded to a nearby couple who watched the exchange with interest and curiosity.

As they waited for the valet parking service, Alecia said, "You may not be, as you so crudely put it, panting for a man, Cary, but at least one seems to have fallen into your lap."

"What can I do?" Cary smirked in exaggeration. "One look at my little red MG and men practically swoon at my feet! He is very handsome, isn't he, and," she added for Phillip's benefit, "he is a practicing physician."

"Be careful driving home," Phillip said, preparing to close her car door.

"Don't worry about me," Cary told him. "I'm stopping to pick up some groceries on my way home."

When she pulled up in front of Rosemary, sometime after eleven, she saw immediately the note. It was a large sheet of paper tacked to the door. What now? she wondered. It had been a long day and dealing with her brother always tired her. Her spirits revived instantly when she read Spence's scrawl: *If you promise not to turn back into a charlady at midnight— or if you want company before then, call . . . Prince Spence.*

She kicked off her shoes and nervously dialed Spence's number. He answered on the first ring. Cary mimicked a princess drawl. "Ms Cinderella here. The prince can come calling, but you'll risk my falling asleep at your feet!"

"I'll risk it," chuckled Spence. "I'll bring a thermos of hot coffee, and I happen to know you have a Mrs. Alison's special buttermilk pie!"

Apparently nothing went unnoticed around here, Cary mused, sliding the pie in the oven to warm.

"Be still my heart," Cary directed as she opened the door. Because her heart was racing wildly. Spence was in light corduroys and a loose pullover, looking as calm as a train at a dead stop.

"No prince thou," she said. "No glass slipper, no majestic robes!" She kept her voice light, determined that he should not know his effect on her.

"Just the perfect Kenyan coffee." He extended the thermos gallantly. "And I could produce paper cups so you won't have to wash up afterwards!"

"Don't you dare! Good coffee deserves at least a good mug," Cary returned. "And the pie is warming even as we speak."

When they had settled themselves in the living room with pie and coffee, Spence said, "I want to apologize for last night. You took me by surprise and I was rude."

Cary busied herself with the pie. Her mouth full, she said, "And I was inquisitive, too nosy for my own good. Let's forget it."

"Agreed."

For the next hour or so, they chatted as if they were old friends. Cary was occasionally aware that his gaze was intense, but she kept the conversation light. She told him that her brother and sister-in-law were in town.

"There's just enough age difference," she said, "to mean that Phillip has taken the childhood admonition 'watch over your little sister' to extremes. He's twelve years older than I. You can imagine his concern when I was a teenager!"

"You're way beyond teenager now," Spence pointed out.

"Well, thanks, mister prince," laughed Cary as Spence recognized his gaffe. She held up a hand in mock horror. "If not 'way beyond, far enough to make my own decisions. But Phillip is slow to change."

"We all have to grow up some time," Spence stated.

Cary continued her thoughts about Phillip. "He and Alecia couldn't believe it when I met Justin tonight," she said.

"Justin?" Spence's tone now held an edge. "When did you meet him?"

At Cary's look of surprise at his brusqueness, Spence said, "None of my business, right? Right. Justin's just getting his practice started. I wouldn't think he'd have time for much else right now."

"He was at the Grove Park with an older couple, and he'd seen me, or my car. He came roaring by in a yellow car that just matches his hair. He seems nice."

Spence looked at his watch and stood, abruptly. "It's late for a working man," he declared. "Unlike the doctors of the city, us country boys gotta get up early." Intent on controlling her thudding pulse, Cary went to the kitchen to retrieve his thermos and handed it to him.

"We finished off half that pie," she commented. "Would you like to take the rest with you? You working guys do need your strength."

Spence declined the pie, but he looked for a moment as if he were tempted to bend and kiss her. Cary knew that if he even stepped close, all her reserve would melt away like sugar in a warm rain. She stepped back, putting some distance between them, and held the door for him. His look was both baffled and restrained, but he smiled and murmured, "Good night, princess."

Around ten o'clock the next morning Cary appeared in ThymeTable's greenhouse. "I'm here to help all the working guys," she announced. She carried her coffee cup in her hand, a chunk of buttered bread in the other.

Her hunter green lightweight khaki slacks belted at the waist accentuated her slimness. Her hair shone in the filtered sunlight. Spence's slow approving appraisal sent shivers down her spine, especially since his eyes lingered on the loose cotton shirt of which she'd left a couple of buttons undone. Abruptly he was all business. He reached under a table and handed her an apron with the words "Farmers Co-op" on it. "You're not quite dressed for this work," he said huskily. "Sure you want to help?"

"I'm not playing the tourist." Cary's eyes sparkled. Just being near him enlivened her every sense.

"You are a paying guest," Spence pointed out, "and a green thumb's not a requirement written into the lease." He was doing something with tiny plants and Cary tied the apron behind her and came over to watch with interest. The greenhouse had long, tables along each side and down the center. The humid air smelled of potting soil.

"Know anything at all about transplanting?" Spence asked.

"Hearts or otherwise?"

He grinned. "Basil, in this case. Hearts are a little more difficult."

"Nothing," she peered at the dozens of tiny plants, "about either."

"Here." Spence handed her a pair of gloves. "Put these on," he ordered. "I always keep an extra pair, just in case some wandering female tenant needs something to do. And I could use some help."

He swept some clutter aside and made a space for her. "A couple of local kids will be here after lunch to work, but my trip put me a little behind."

If the trip had to do with Darla, Cary wasn't about to question him. In fact, she thought, maybe I am still irritated about his "none of your business" crack. But she wouldn't let that interfere with her cheerful mood or the morning's work. Smiling sweetly, she gestured at the table, "Just tell me what to do, oh landlord, and I am your serf for the morning."

Spence instructed her in the intricacies of getting the basil seedlings from the bed into the small boxes. As they worked through the morning, she was aware of his physical presence, his clean odor, his masculinity, and she was careful not to brush against him. Today he was in faded jeans, jeans that rode his hips comfortably. A gray sweatshirt with cutoff sleeves revealed muscular arms and shapely wrists, and, she noted, a Rolex watch. When their fingers touched as he showed her how to gently remove the plants, she drew back quickly. Let him think she disliked his touch; she knew she distrusted herself. "That way disaster lies," she again reminded herself.

Their silence was companionable and the only exchange for some time concerned the plants and how she was to handle them. Spence, totally engrossed in what he was doing, stopped only to instruct or enlighten her.

"Basil's called the royal herb by the French, but it's had a mixed reputation from the earliest known writers on herbs," he said. "In Eastern countries it's revered, and Indians used to put sprigs of the plant on their dead to protect them from potential evils of the other world." He worked methodically, his every move efficient. "On the other hand, early western writers claimed it had an affinity for poison and grew best if the planting were accompanied by lots of loud cursing. Want to try a few curses to make it thrive?"

"These little plants seem to be thriving already. You must have turned the air blue when you planted the seeds!"

"I gave the kids permission to do their worst when they

did it. So I take no credit, except for 'planting the seed' in their heads." He laughed.

"All I know about basil is it rhymes with "dazzle," and I usually toss some into anything tomatoey I'm cooking. Never seems to hurt."

"It also supposedly helps tomatoes outside the cooking pot. Some people swear that planting basil around their tomatoes wards off pests and disease. And it does seem to enhance the taste of tomatoes it grows near."

Some two hours later, Spence began cleaning up. "We'll have a space at the Herb Fair, just when these are ready to plant. Basil's a good seller."

As he returned tools, buckets, trowels to their locations, Cary skinned off her gloves, washed her hands, and leaned back contentedly. She was a little tired from having bent over the work table too long. Spence noticed.

"You overdid it, didn't you? I shouldn't have let you work like that!"

"I'm fine," she declared. "Please don't get into the habit of deciding for me what I did or overdid!"

Hardly knowing why she had found his solicitous tone annoying rather than endearing, she said, "Phillip's watching out for my interests. One male doing that is all I can take."

Even as she said it, she wondered if Phillip's visit had more to do with business than with brotherly concern. A frown furrowed her brow. Phillip and his deals! Just what was he doing in the western part of the state?

Spence was watching her closely and she erased the worry from her eyes and avoided his while she industriously moved a few items into, if a not more orderly arrangement, at least a different one.

"Wouldn't most girls—" Spence quickly amended, "most women be happy to have a concerned brother? You seem awfully touchy about a simple visit."

Spence scrubbed up at the sink. "I suppose they are right to be concerned about your well being." He continued with a smile, "Although you seem to have had lots of energy yesterday. Photographing all morning and partying all evening."

"My left foot tires easily," Cary told him, choosing to ignore both the partying comment and her own misgivings about Phillip and Alecia's arrival. "I had back surgery," she told him as they walked toward Rosemary. "No real problem," she assured him lightly, "but the family frets.

I hardly notice anymore. It's simply a matter of time."

Spence nodded, "I would offer my arm in true gentlemanly fashion, but you'd likely snap my head off and decline, but if you need . . ."

"Thanks, but no, no thanks."

At the cottage, Cary felt exactly like a princess who had been seen home by her gallant suitor. "I liked working in the greenhouse. I'd like to photograph the progress of the basil as it comes along, pick out a pet plant and record its growth. I've never done anything like that."

"Sure. Make yourself at home around here. If you want, notice I didn't say NEED, my help rigging up lighting or anything, I am your ever-present, never-failing landlord and your wish is my command!"

"Great. See you later."

Cary made herself a fluffy omelet with fresh green peppers and Swiss cheese, and ate hungrily. Then she settled down with a pot of ThymeTable's special tea for a restful afternoon of reading up on basil. When she heard a car outside, her first thought was that Phillip and Alecia were visiting again; her second was that their Buick didn't sound quite so clattery.

"Anybody home?" Justin poked his blond head in the front door. "Oops, I'm interrupting! Study time?"

Cary uncurled herself from the sofa. It was impossible to

resist his flashing good-natured grin. "Come in. I'm just reading up on herbs, especially basil. It's a mixed up herb! Supposed to help induce abortions and also believed to be an
aphrodisiac?" She motioned toward the easy chair. "Let me
read you this wonderful sentence: 'As it helps the deficiency
of Venus in one kind, so it spoils all her actions in another.'
And the writer goes on, 'I dare write no more of it.'"

"Hooked already, huh?" Justin didn't seem inclined to
discuss the qualities of an herb. He lowered his well-propor-
tioned frame into the chair. Are all the males around here so
good-looking? Cary wondered. Apparently he was used to
the admiring glances of patients, nurses, and receptionists
and took her welcome for granted.

"Hooked on the country air," Cary said. "I thought I was a
flatlander, but I love it here." "You're from up in Virginia, I
think Dad said." Justin stretched out. "Here on a vacation."

"Yes, from Barrymore, about three hundred miles from
here."

"I know where it is. Nice town. Lots of old money there. I
went to the University of Virginia and did my medical training at Roanoke."

"Mary told me a little about your Dad. He's not ill?"

"He's fair to middling as they say around here." Justin's
eyes betrayed his concern. "Actually he's failing. He simply
forgets or is too stubborn to take the medicine I prescribe for
his arthritis. So I come down as often as possible to check on
him. He's also diabetic and his pancreas is wearing out. He
does take his insulin, but he's stubborn as a mule about watching his diet carefully."

Justin explained further about Robert's condition, and
then he exclaimed, "Enough medical talk. At least enough
about Dad. He's a very private person. But," Justin grinned,
"we can talk about me as much as you like!"

Cary liked his exuberance and his cockiness; she could
sense that few women resisted his charm. Then tell me about

your practice. How long have you been out of med school? Do you have a private practice or are you with a group or clinic?"

"I'm in with a large family practice clinic in Fairmont. Just started with them nine months ago, and, as most new MDs can tell you, I'm hardly making a fortune yet!"

"Hence the vehicle out front?" Cary couldn't resist the jab.

"Right! It took me through school and through residency and it'll have to take me through the lean times til most of my debts are paid off. I admit the other physicians ask me to park it on the far side of the doctors' parking lot!"

Cary laughed.

"Just kidding," Justin added. "Before you know it, I'll be a Jaguar man! That MG out there must have set you back some big bucks. It's neat."

"Then let's take it for a drive," Cary invited. "You can drive it. I'd love to go up on the Parkway."

"You're on. I can put that baby through its paces the way it's meant to be driven."

"I'll get a scarf. We can put the top down."

"Why don't I call Dad and tell him we'll bring something for dinner and you can meet him?" Justin started for the telephone. "Since I'm here for such a short time."

"Sure. I like a dutiful son." Cary came back with scarf and light jacket. "And I'd love to meet him."

The drive on the Blue Ridge Parkway was spectacular and thrilling. The two-lane highway running from Staunton, Virginia, to near Cherokee, North Carolina, hugs the sides of mountains, running across ridges, with scenic viewing areas every few miles. Both had been on the Parkway, but it was a perfect day for a drive: no wind, light traces of greenery showing everywhere, but leaving space to actually see into the forest. Later in the summer, heavy foliage would obscure the inner view. True to his prediction, Justin handled the MG beautifully.

"You drive like a true Englishman," Cary complimented him.

"It's these magnificent surgeon's hands," Justin held both hands in the air for a moment. "I suppose they're wasted in family practice."

"Surely a good doctor isn't wasted anywhere. Are you having second thoughts or harboring secret thoughts of being a surgeon?"

"There's certainly more money in surgery," Justin said. "Let's stop at this overlook. That's the Asheville watershed down there." He pointed to a shining body of water in the valley below. As they stood admiring the scene, he casually draped his arm around her shoulders.

Cary enjoyed the long afternoon immensely. It was getting chilly as they drove back into town and stopped to order Chinese food to go.

"Dad's pretty much a vegetarian," Justin commented, collecting the steamed vegetables, rice, moo gai pan. "Can you carry our sweet and sour pork and the soup?"

Robert Moreland was tall, very thin, slightly stooped. His completely white hair was longish and thinning, his eyes the same bright blue as his son's. He welcomed Cary warmly, extending his hand and leading them inside. The house was a modest frame structure on one floor, and the inside, where a fire burned in the rock fireplace, was a comfortable mix of masculine and bookish clutter. The table was perfectly laid with good silver and cloth napkins.

"I didn't expect such niceties with take-out food!" Cary exclaimed.

Justin clapped his Dad on the shoulders. "One of his quirks is the absolute refusal to use paper napkins. You won't find one in the house. And if you use cloth napkins, you might as well use the family silver."

"That's about all that's left of the family fortune," Robert stated as he brought a pitcher of water to the table. "And it's yours, Just, whenever you decide to settle down."

"Whoa, Dad, I've got a few good years of bachelorhood left in me yet." Justin was unperturbed by the remark, and Cary assumed it was not the first time Robert had hinted at his son's unmarried state.

"And do I have a few good years left to be a doting grand-father in?" Robert asked gravely.

"Come on, Dad, let's not get morbid." Justin brought the food, now in various mismatched bowls, to the table.

"I'll just put the kettle on for tea. Dad always sits facing the door, so, Cary, you can sit there," he directed.

During the meal, Robert was the gracious host; he had the built-in reserve of a scholar who knows much more than he intends to impart and who chooses his words carefully to make the most of each utterance. He had a reputation of sorts as a "finder" of old books, he admitted, and did most of the searching by telephone and fax machine. He seldom left his home.

"It's hard to find many places like this," he said. "A lot of families are breaking up their acreage as the older members die. We were lucky to get this large old family farm a few years ago. Now almost every hillside's been leveled or faces the prospect of being dotted with vacation retreats or worse— the worse being condominium or golf complexes."

Justin's glance at Cary told her this, too, was not a new complaint. "Bear with him," his look said.

"We've managed to hold on to these thirty-odd acres," Robert groused. "And we, I, at least, intend to keep hanging on, even," here he cast a glance at Justin, "if it means selling the family silver!"

Justin shrugged. "Whatever it takes, Dad. After all, I got through school without that ultimate sacrifice. I'll be on easy street in a few years! Seriously, though, the Cove's not in financial trouble, is it? You're making the mortgage payments?"

"So far, son, so far." Robert suddenly sounded tired and looked older than his seventy-four years. "But Agnes and Alice are getting on and so am I."

"No need to worry yet, for God's sake," Justin was irritated. "All of you are still here. Let's have some tea."

He and Cary both jumped up to head for the kitchen. "No, let me get it," he said. "You keep Dad company, and try to find something pleasant to talk about!"

While Justin was in the kitchen, the telephone rang. Robert answered and winked at Cary as he muttered, "Yes. Here. Yes. Fine." When he hung up, he said, "That was your landlord, wondering if you were here. Worried, I guess."

After tea and fortune cookies and conversation about books, Cary's college, anecdotes about the gruesomeness of medical studies, and the goats of Agnes and Alice, Cary realized it was almost midnight.

"Look at the time! I'm keeping late hours these days." Thinking of Spence's Cinderella comment and suddenly getting a lurch in her stomach, she went on, "I might turn into a pumpkin if I'm not back at Rosemary pretty soon."

"I'll drive you over and get my car," Justin said.

"Thank you. Robert, I'm sure we'll see more of each other. I'll be at ThymeTable for a while yet."

"Enjoyed the evening, Cary." At the door, Robert took her hand with old-fashioned courtesy. "Chinese food always tastes better in the presence of a lovely young lady, and I can't remember when any tasted so good."

Cary touched Justin lightly on the shoulder as she told him she'd had a wonderful time. He was leaning toward her and she thus prevented any more romantic gesture on his part.

"Let's try for a repeat then," he suggested gracefully.

"Maybe. We'll be in touch." She dashed up her steps.

As Cary snuggled into sleep under a down comforter, a small smile stayed with her. Her landlord had been worried about her. Good for him.

Chapter 4

"No," Cary assured her Mother, "I'm not at all lonesome."

"Darling," her Mother said, "Smith is bringing some young friend home from upstate New York."

Cary smiled. Her brother had his gossip straight.

"It's time he settled down, I suppose," her mother continued. "After all, his father's retiring within a year or so."

Cary said firmly, "Mother, we meant next to nothing to each other. I hope you can soon give him my congratulations on an engagement!"

She stretched contentedly on the sofa. Twisting her foot in the air, Cary realized that in only a few days, its tautness had subsided considerably.

"Oh, dear, it's too soon surely for that." Her mother hesitated briefly, "And Lanny . . . . "

"Lanny has hardly crossed my mind these days. It's over with us."

Cary knew that Ruthlene had regarded her daughter's infatuation with Lanny as a temporary folly. If she now felt that her opinion had been validated, she said only, "You sound so much better, Cary. So alive and happy."

"I'm learning all about herbs and maybe something about me out here," Cary laughed. "Maybe I'm really cut out to be a farmer."

When Cary asked about Phillip's visit, Ruthlene Randall replied that she supposed Phillip was simply concerned about his sister. Cary knew that her mother paid relatively little attention to business matters. She had never had to concern herself. She trusted implicitly both her husband and her son.

Shaking off her doubts about Phillip, Cary loaded color film in her camera and went picture-looking. It was almost four o'clock when she meandered back to the cultivated beds at ThymeTable. "Meander" was a word she liked and this meandering afternoon had been a good one. Today she'd photographed dozens of wild flowers, tiny and close to the ground. Next, she would photograph them in close up black and white, to capture the contrast in textures, the density of moss against the delicate flowers.

Her cheeks glowed with the exertion of walking—meandering—all afternoon. In a Wordsworthian mood she declaimed loudly, "One impulse from a vernal wood may teach you more of man, of moral evil and of good than all the sages can!"

"Do you do that often?" a voice asked, as she rounded the corner of one of the out buildings.

Spence sat on the step in the slanting sunlight. With his arms on his knees he appeared pensive and withdrawn, his smile forced.

"Do what?"

"Talk to yourself? Actually I recognize the voice of the old Laker himself," Spence rubbed his head. "I suppose I shouldn't be surprised. Last summer Mrs. Brown went around citing birth and death dates of all her ancestors. Must be something in the tea!"

"That makes us all want to spout?"

Spence threw her his denim jacket and Cary settled herself on the grass nearby. There wasn't room for both to sit comfortably on the rickety steps. He didn't shift to invite her closer.

"It is an annoying habit I have, but I do it usually 'in the bliss of solitude.' You startled me."

"Sorry."

"I've been photographing everything in sight." She told him about her day. His "Uh-huns" and "Yeahs" were perfunctory. He might have been memorizing the tree line on the distant mountains or picturing the Atlantic some six hundred miles beyond. As silent as a painted ship upon a painted ocean, she thought. For some moments neither spoke.

While his stare was directed at the faraway peaks, Cary indulged in the pleasure of looking at him, the shirt pulled tight about the shoulders, the silver medallion gleaming, his set jaw, his tousled brown hair. She gave herself a shake, warding off the sensual warmth that just looking at Spence set in motion.

"I'm going to run into town and leave some film to be developed." She stood up.

He appeared not to have heard.

"Oh," she grinned impishly. "Thanks for worrying about me last night."

Spence's lips tightened. "I can't have my tenant disappearing, can I?"

"Oh, come on!" Cary couldn't believe what she was hearing. "You're not going to check up on me every night, are you?"

"I might if I'm worried about you."

She tossed his jacket to him. "You're carrying this landlord responsibility 'way beyond reason."

Spence looked sheepish. He stood, rubbing his hand through his hair in a conciliatory gesture. "Want some company going to town?"

"In your grumpy mood?"

"You might need some help, especially if you were to end up in a ditch again."

Cary's face darkened. The "need" word again. "If you'd like to come with me—for the pleasure of my company, you're welcome. If you're offering because you think it's your duty, forget it!"

He threw up his hands in mock surrender. "It's purely the pleasure of your company, ma'am. We can grab a bit to eat somewhere."

Cary quickly slipped on soft moccasins and a clean tee shirt and ran a comb through her hair while Spence lounged on the porch. In spite of his words, she felt Spence was merely being dutiful. Something had been weighing heavily on his mind. Their banter had roused him from it, but this deliberate reserve hadn't been there the first night at ThymeTable.

They ate double veggie burgers and fries at the local Backyard Burgers and smacked their lips appreciatively. But conversation did not flow easily.

"It's still early," Cary said. "Would you like to meet my brother and his wife? They probably haven't gone to dinner yet."

She couldn't quite diagnose Spence's look, but when he said, "Sure," she fished her phone from the glove compartment.

"They say to come over to the lobby. They have dinner reservations in about thirty minutes, but they're curious to meet my landlord."

"And I'm curious to meet Phillip Randall," returned Spence flatly.

In a few moments they entered the well-lighted lobby and Cary led the way to the waiting Phillip and Alecia.

"Glad to meet you, Spence." Phillip, in gray double-breasted suit and red striped tie, extended his hand in his best businessman manner. Alecia murmured appropriate words of greeting while her eyes glistened. Alecia had the ability to make every man, even the pillars of the community, soften with pleasure at her adoring gaze. Spence, however, hardly softened; in fact, he was little more than civil.

"We're meeting some people in a few minutes, but how about a drink at the bar?" Phillip invited.

"Thanks, but we'll be getting back to the farm," replied Spence. Cary didn't want to linger over drinks either, but surely Spence could have given her an opportunity to consider the invitation. Alecia gave a minute shrug as she looked from one to the other. Cary could hear the story back in Barrymore: "The man was in such a rush to get Cary (laugh) back to the farm!"

Phillip was saying, "Spence Bradford. The name rings a bell. Where?"

He broke off as a middle-aged couple came through the door. "Here are our guests, Cary. Good to meet you, Bradford. Now if you'll excuse us." He shook Spence's hand again and tucked Alecia's arm through his as they strode confidently across the lobby.

"They certainly didn't intend to introduce us to their friends!" Cary said as they settled into her car. "Think it's because I'm not presentable enough?"

Spence wrenched the wheel sharply. "Stop fishing for compliments. I didn't need any introduction. That was Joey Pullman and his wife. I know them well enough."

"Oh. Then is there something I don't know?"

"Just why is Phillip here, Cary?"

Cary's head snapped up at his abruptness and the question itself.

"What do you think?" she parried defensively.

"I think it's a hell of a lot more than brotherly concern." He reversed the car and accelerated so quickly that Cary almost hit her head on the rearview mirror.

"You mean some business deal?"

"More than just some deal," he said curtly. "And you don't know anything about it?"

She heard the unspoken question: would you tell me if you did? And in her defensiveness, her own doubts about Phillip's presence must have shown. Still, she didn't know anything. And just what loyalty did she owe to Spence and to ThymeTable?

"He said he was worried about me. That's all I know."

"Umm," he grunted.

The tension as they drove back to the farm was evident in Spence's tightlipped silence and his short comments when Cary tried to make conversation. Cary was baffled and growing irritable. If he had a problem, why didn't he say so. This thundercloud sitting beside her was oppressive. As if in complete accord, the thunderclouds that had been accumulating overhead since dark and now completely covered the moon opened up. The beating rain outside and

Spence's suppressed anger increased the tension in the vehicle. Cary glanced sideways at Spence just as a bolt of lightning zigzagged across the sky. She giggled nervously.

Slamming on the brakes in front of Rosemary, Spence jumped out. "Come on, I'll see you to the door!"

It was only a few feet but without umbrella or rain gear, they were drenched in those few steps. Spence had grasped Cary's arm as he opened the door and he held it tightly as he faced her. His eyes blazed.

"I'm sure you think it's funny," he ground out. "A family joke. Con the jerk, is that the game you're playing?"

Cary yanked her arm away. She wanted to slap his face, his streaming face, not more than inches from hers. She willed herself to calm down and in her lack of response, the moment of absolute stillness caught both of them. Her body swayed a fraction toward him; he stepped forward and his arms went round her. She could hardly breathe against his wet chest and her heart thumped so loudly that surely only the driving rain prevented his hearing it.

"Ah, Cary, I thought I could trust you, I wanted to trust you!"

She pulled back at the words, strangely contradictory to his fierce hold. His hand cupped her chin tightly and raised it. Before she could protest, before she could question, he rasped, "I don't have to trust you. Right now I want you."

His lips descended, hard. Cary jerked her head to one side, and his mouth hardly grazed hers.

"You're despicable! You talk in riddles and you announce you want me. Am I supposed to guess what you mean or fall into your arms?"

"You can tell what I mean," he said, his voice a sneer.

She was still pressed against him and there was no mistaking his desire.

Lightning flashed close by, and in its brightness, Spence must have seen the astonishment on Cary's face as he had surely sensed her desire moments before. He released her abruptly, stepped back, and rubbed his hands down his sides. His face became a bland mask.

Cary shivered both from the cold rain and from the insinuation in his voice and the implication from his body. She closed her eyes and deliberately counted silently to ten to regain some control over her voice and her feelings. She said tightly, "I'm afraid I do see what you mean. Goodnight."

She only wanted to get away from his presence and try to sort out his words and his actions. And she didn't intend to let him see how hurt she was that she had misjudged him.

"No, you don't. Let's go inside," Spence said. "It's cold out here. I'll try to explain."

"There is no need to explain." Cary felt like a statue turning to dough; her control was deserting her, flooding away like the stream gushing down the driveway. If she dissolved, she wanted to be alone, not before his speculative eyes.

"I certainly won't invite you in. Just leave." She was inside the door, clearly intending to close it in his face.

"Wait, Cary, I need to . . ."

"You don't need to explain. I don't need you." She was close to tears, whether of anger or disillusionment she wasn't sure. "I don't need anything from you."

She closed the door quietly, definitively, and marveled at how loudly the inside latch clicked.

Some minutes later she heard the door of his vehicle slam; he must have stood on the porch of Rosemary before braving the storm again. Probably waiting, Cary thought, for me to come out and apologize. Apologize for what? What evil plot was she supposed to be a part of? He clearly considered her the villain, somehow connected with Phillip, but surely—in a less heated moment—she could clear up any confusion in that direction. She was less sure of clearing the confusion she felt inside. She shivered, cold and vacant, because of his distrust. She would have returned his kiss hungrily if his words hadn't jarred her. Call it what it is, Cary, she admonished herself. It's sex appeal, pure and simple. And sex appeal, she assured herself, I can handle. Forget how good and right his body fit against yours. Forget your answering quickening breath. Remember his sneer and his arrogance. Remembering warmed her and rekindled her anger. She picked up the herb book and threw it with a resounding crash against the wall. Being at ThymeTable Farm wasn't nearly as peaceful and serene as she'd thought.

Chapter 5

The next few days Cary alternated between thinking and doing, between serene contentment and questioning her contentment, between resolving to break with her life in Barrymore and wondering if she really belonged at ThymeTable.

Sometimes she and Mary took the MG and drove for hours along back road into neighboring counties to explore waterfalls mostly. Mary laughingly admitted that being from the Midwest might explain her "waterfall fixation." She gloried in getting as close as possible and usually burst into some German or French aria with the enthusiasm of a water nymph. Startled tourists gaped as Mary spread her arms and sang joyfully and loudly. Cary used the waterfall expeditions to good advantage, getting excellent shots from a variety of wet and spraying angles. In the unpredictable manner of spring and in seeming accord with her mood swings, the rains alternated with blindingly bright hours of sunlight. She understood why the mountains to the west were named Smoky by early settlers; quite often their crests were shrouded like ladies discreetly wrapped in filmy shawls. More rain than sunshine found its way through the mist and clouds, though, and the overall effect was damp. Sometimes Cary felt as if she were living in the soak cycle of a washing machine. In more poetic moments she remembered Wordsworth's "The earth, and every common sight . . . did seem appareled in celestial light,/The glory and the freshness of a dream."

Perhaps because looking through her camera's lens sharpened her vision and perception, Cary saw spring with both an inward eye and an outward appreciation. She slogged through mud and wet weeds to photograph at random the minute and the magnificent. In the local gift shops photographs of the mountains abounded, yet she couldn't resist trying long shots through the gardens and closeups of rain drops clinging to blackberry vines.

When not taking pictures or just tramping in the wetness, Cary visited with Mary and the sisters. Mary was facing a deadline for a major translating project, however, and was worried about it or about something. Alice and Agnes showed her numerous "medicines" they concocted for their minor ailments, always insisting that for them they worked.

Robert reported that Justin's clinic had called him back to work when a senior physician suffered a heart attack. In a scruffy sweater, a scarf wound round his neck, and hunched over a book catalog, Robert appeared much thinner and frailer than he had earlier. Cary thought that Justin's blondness and debonair laughter would have seemed out of place in the cold dampness.

Cary's hours out of doors were doubled by the time inside. Cozy, cocooned in her cottage, she read her herb books extensively. She didn't want to ask herself why she found the herb world fascinating. After all, she'd read enough novels and romances and she needed something else. Certainly she was in no mood for romances—or romance.

Spence did not call. Mary implied that he was gone on business or had dashed off for some reason. Cary asked no questions. She kept busy partly as a way of insulating herself from remembering the charms, the sex appeal, of her landlord.

When she didn't hear from Phillip and Alecia, she reluctantly called their hotel. She felt, after all, that she was their "hostess" in the western part of the state, but Alecia quickly disabused her of that attitude.

"Darling, don't worry about us. Phillip is very busy just now. Shall I have him call?" Alecia said.

"No. No. Thanks, Alecia, you're a dear." Cary hung up thinking wickedly that at that moment she sounded just like Alecia.

Johnny knocked on the door. "Just delivering some of Mrs. Alison's bread and some magazines from Mom. It's too wet to get out or I'd suggest a sightseeing expedition."

"Johnny, I'm having a wonderful time, believe it or not!" Cary flipped through the glossy pages. "These look great. I'm not familiar with any of them."

"Well, if you get bored, just give us a ring. Oh, Mom said to check out page ten in the dining magazine."

Page ten announced the magazine's third annual amateur original recipe/original photography contest. Cary read with interest and decided she needed a challenge. She certainly didn't count herself a cook but she could follow a recipe and she could take pictures. A bachelor uncle whom she'd once complimented on his culinary ability had told her, "If you can read, you can cook. And I can read."

The next day, Cary went to the city library and studied the previous contest winners in earlier issues of the magazine. Deadline was almost a month away. At the rate her social life was going now, that gave her plenty of time. She began to experiment with the herbs in the pantry, choosing very simple dishes, concentrating on appetizers and desserts. The knack, she thought, is to keep the recipe simple, give it an unusual name, and photograph it perfectly. No small knack. She had to read up more on indoor shooting. She was getting to be a regular at the library and at Malaprops Bookstore near it.

As Cary kept active, she was sorting out her feelings for Lanny and what had attracted her to him. He was her delayed reaction, perhaps, to the "behave nicely, don't embarrass the family, act like a lady" code which bundled her through school and protected her beyond. She had been enwrapped safely in the sweet shawls of her family and community like the distant Smoky Mountains were wrapped in a filmy mist. Perhaps through Lanny she asserted her independence. Maybe she'd chosen him rather than admit that her college degree had not provided her with enough stimulus to find truly engrossing work. For the first time Cary articulated to herself that she had refused to see the real Lanny. Choosing to view his crude mannerisms as refreshing indifference to the mores of her community, she had romanticized him: the Byronic hero, "mad, bad, and dangerous to know."

At any rate she had closed the door on her life of only a few weeks ago. But she wasn't sure what door she was opening—life, love, or a combination of both.

In her trips to Asheville, Cary also explored the downtown with its array of banks and churches, its art and craft shops. She found a Mountain Mark Photography Studio that advertised rental dark rooms complete with all equipment. Now she felt ready—and she certainly had the time—to get serious about printing her own film. She met the retired photographer, Mark Coleman, who ran the business, and within the hour she signed a lease for one of the darkrooms and for advanced instruction in developing film. Her days took on an intensely satisfying routine: mornings photographing or experimenting with simple dishes; afternoons in the darkroom for three or four hours; evenings reading or visiting Mary, the Grayson sisters, or Mrs. Alison.

Before Phillip and Alecia left the area, the three of them

had a rather unsatisfactory luncheon. Cary sensed an undercurrent in the conversation that disturbed her.

"Who're the Pullmans?" she inquired. "Did you enjoy
your evening with them?"

"Pullman of Pullman-Bowles," Phillip answered shortly.
"You've surely noticed their office building near here. Real-
tors."

"Phillip, you are here on business, aren't you? More developments, more golf courses, more timeshares?" Cary's
frown signaled her disapproval. She remembered the shock
when she'd seen the swath of bulldozing at Suntip Beach.
The neat rows of condominiums that met her eye on the
next visit did not eradicate the sense of what had been lost to
create the model village with its new pavement, new shrub-
bery, new identity.

"For God's sake, Cary, grow up."

"Yes, dear," Alecia said patronizingly. "We are here on
business. And to see you, of course."

And, thought Cary, you'll write the whole trip off as business expenses.

"There's plenty of untouched acreage out there," Phillip
went on, "plenty of room for another golf course. Statistics
show that more and more people want to live in the relative
safety of the mountains rather than risk the dangers of hurri-
canes at the shore." He shrugged carelessly. "And that's fine
with me. The problem is getting some of these folks to part
with their land."

"Money talks," Alecia said.

In that moment, in the look that passed between Phillip
and Alecia, Cary knew they were talking not just land in general but a specific parcel of land. A frisson passed through
her. She opened her mouth to protest, to ask, to declare . . .
but what? She felt queasy.

Forcing herself to speak quietly, after a pause, Cary asked,
"Are you talking about ThymeTable Farm?"

Again a shrug from Phillip. "Not to worry, little sister. It's no concern of yours at the moment."

"Or at all," contributed Alecia. "Cary, dear, you are only renting out there."

Cary was dizzied by the shock to her system. Phillip, the sneak, realizing where she was, had undoubtedly checked land values. What had he discovered that brought him, with such brotherly concern for her well-being, so quickly to Asheville? Was Spence in financial difficulties? Was ThymeTable in danger? Was the entire cove? Now she remembered a comment about bankers, Mary's worried frown, Spence's withdrawn pensiveness in the afternoon and then his tightlipped anger the night they'd come into town. ThymeTable's herb beds tackled by bulldozers and smashed by huge dump trucks, a blacktopped highway. Yes, the area was a natural for development, lying cupped at the base of a mountain. Just how far up the mountain would the condos extend?

Alecia, alarmed at Cary's suddenly pale face, spoke in a sharp, businesslike tone. "Nothing is settled yet. You'll be back in Barrymore long before anything's . . ."

"Phillip! Why?" burst out Cary. "I thought you were all tied up with that Suntip project. How can you take on something else when Suntip's not—"

"Suntip's not your problem. And neither is this project."

Cary noted with dismay his use of the word "project." That meant he was more than just looking around. He had a definite plan, seeking investors, getting his intentions established, building a local base. Probably in the last few days, he and Alecia had dined and met with as many influential "movers and shakers" as they could line up.

"But, Phillip, I want to know." Cary insisted. "Is ThymeTable for sale?"

Phillip's eyes hardened. "There is nothing you have

to know. Period. Finish your coffee, Alecia, we have to be somewhere at two o'clock."

The next few minutes passed in silence. Cary knew she'd get nothing further from them. Phillip paid the check and they left the restaurant.

"We're leaving tomorrow, Cary. So we'll see you in Barrymore in a few weeks," Phillip was as bland as if they'd been discussing new carpet or drapes.

"Yes," Alecia smiled. "Surely you'll be ready to return to work by then. How long can you occupy yourself out here?"

Cary's good manners required her to say goodby, thanks for lunch, and hello to Mom and Dad, but she was fuming as she slid into her car. She really wanted to simply slap Alecia, to wipe that smug look off their faces.

She couldn't drive straight back to ThymeTable and ask what is going on. She had her appointment at two o'clock also, to work at Mountain Mark. And besides Spence was not at ThymeTable. And Mary was busy. Her distracted look was probably not so much about her translation deadline as about the farm. Why hadn't she said anything?

For three hours, in the darkroom Cary forced herself to think composition, to crop photographs judiciously, to experiment cautiously, to listen to Mark Coleman's critiques and calm advice. She was moderately proud of her black and white prints as she finally stood back and viewed them objectively. The closeups of the goats were lively, the mischief gleamed in their eyes, their coats were perfectly highlighted. Some of her closeups of flowers needed much more work. But, on the whole, she was satisfied with her progress.

"Thanks, Mark." She gathered up her shoulder bag and portfolio. "I'll be back day after tomorrow to play around more with what I worked on today. And I may have another roll ready to print."

"Same time, Friday then." Mark made a note on his calendar. "This rain getting to you?" he inquired.

"No. No. Not the rain." Cary smiled unconvincingly. Not the rain, she thought, but not anything I can talk about.

"You're doing fine, Cary. You have a natural eye," Mark assured her.

"Thanks. See you Friday."

Cary mulled over Phillip's comments as she prepared her evening meal. Mary had given her a recipe for vegetable barley soup with various herbs tossed in. Could she call the Pullmans and simply ask what her brother was up to? In her experience, businessmen could be utterly pleasant and surprisingly tight-mouthed at the same time. Both Phillip and her father could defuse questions without revealing anything significant and without hurting feelings (or business). No, a direct approach would not work. Perhaps she could go into Pullman- Bowles and apply for a job. If Mr. Pullman didn't see her for a few days, it might work. She could find out what was in the plans. Be sensible, she told herself, it's very likely that Mr. Pullman would interview all applicants, if even a job were available, and he'd certainly recognize her name. Be even more sensible, Cary thought, and face it: it's not your concern and if Spence wanted you to know . . .

She put her spoon aside as the realization hit her. Did Spence think she did know? Did he think she had told her brother about ThymeTable? What could she have told him? Did he think they were in some sort of conspiracy? That would explain his questions and his behavior when last she saw him. Tears of frustration welled up in Cary's eyes. She felt helpless and confused. Spence didn't trust her, probably Mary didn't quite trust her, maybe Alice, Agnes, and even Robert wondered about her sudden appearance at the farm.

I can't sit moping here, doing nothing even if it's raining outside, Cary decided. A few minutes later she was mopping the kitchen floor.

The telephone jangled in the stillness. She discarded

her rubber gloves and went to answer, her heart pounding as she expected to hear Spence's voice.

"Hello." The feminine voice was sultry and yet contained. "Is Spence Bradford there?"

"No," answered Cary. At the silence on the other end, she asked, "Can I take a message?"

"When do you expect him?"

"Well, unh," Cary mumbled, "I don't expect him. But if it's an emergency, I'll—"

"Do you know where he can be reached?"

"Why should I know?" Cary spoke sharply. "If there's no message," she hesitated, waiting for a clue. When the silence lengthened, she demanded, "Who is this?"

"This is Darla. No message." The line went dead.

The sun shot its "timorous rays" through the windows and bathed Cary in light long before she roused herself. Following Darla's call she'd spent the evening mopping the spotless bathroom floor, cleaning the oven, and wiping the meticulous windowsills until the paint almost cried out in pain. She'd schemed and plotted a dozen totally ridiculous scenarios in which somehow she'd confronted the Pullmans, her family, Spence, Darla . . . and with every one she scrubbed more furiously. She didn't even know Darla's last name! She didn't know where Spence was. She didn't know if he wanted her help, whatever help she could give. She didn't know if he even wanted her at the farm.

Finally after midnight, rummaging around in a kitchen drawer, she found a recipe for Tea to Sleep By and concocted a double serving. Sometime after three a.m. (she kept an eye on the bedside clock), she slept but the tea surely must have also been Tea to Dream By, for her dreams featured giant bulldozers turning teapots, mops, and hillsides into sludge and brownies.

A siren jarred her totally awake, and she leapt from bed to see an ambulance race by, its lights flashing. She dialed

Mary's number but no one answered there or at the Grayson sisters. Robert's number was busy. Cary hurriedly pulled on her jogging outfit. Mary's car screeched to a halt near the door.

"Robert's pretty bad. The paramedics think it's a stroke. They're taking him to the hospital. Johnny and I will go with them," she shouted to Cary. "No, there's really nothing you can do. Justin's on his way. We'll call as soon as we know anything definite."

Cary hurried up to be with Alice and Agnes. Alice had taken Robert some goat cheese and found him collapsed in the kitchen. She'd called Mary and the ambulance and Justin.

Cary and the sisters spent the day waiting, doing a few chores to take their minds off Robert's illness. They intended to go visit as soon as Mary reported that Robert was out of the intensive care unit.

However, the call came in late afternoon that Robert had not recovered consciousness and had died before his son arrived. Then Mary and Johnny returned, their faces haggard. They reported that Justin would be along later.

In the days following, Mary made several calls trying to get in touch with Spence. Cary mourned for Robert and helped her neighbors and Justin as much as she could. She also spent the sunny afternoon hours weeding the herb beds. She listened as Justin talked of his Dad and their life together in the city after his Mother died. He talked dispassionately, a touch cynically about the "good life" that Robert had enjoyed with his books and catalogs. She offered to go with him to the memorial service in the hometown church of his grandparents, but Justin declined, knowing he would be surrounded by relatives.

"It'll be a small service in the church where he and Mother were married, outside Chicago. Lots of cousins," Justin said, kissing her lightly on the forehead. "Lots of family, no money. I'll be back in a few days to pack up. Can't miss too much time at the clinic."

Then he said, "Got word this morning. Spence will fly out to be at the service." Cary felt a surge of pure longing at the sound of Spence's name. She gave Justin's hand an encouraging squeeze. The old Volvo rattled down the drive.

"Justin probably won't spend another two nights in this Cove," Mary said, leaning against the porch railing. She looked drawn and tired. "Come on in the house for awhile, Cary."

"MaryMom, you've got to get some rest now and stop worrying," Johnny hugged her. "I'm going over to Suzanne's."

"You don't think Justin will be back, at least for vacations?" asked Cary.

Mary's gaze was speculative. Was she wondering if Cary and Justin were getting involved? Or was she wondering about Cary's interest in Spence and the farm? In the silence, Cary was uncomfortable with Mary's seeming wariness and reticence.

"Can't you tell me what's bothering you, Mary? I thought we were friends, yet I'm getting the feeling that I'm very much an outsider." Cary's voice trembled slightly. The stress of dealing with Robert's death must be getting to all of us, she thought.

"I don't want to break any confidences, I mean, I don't know if Spence would want me to . . . " Mary stopped, obviously searching for words that wouldn't insult or hurt Cary.

"Spence thinks I'm not to be trusted?"

"Spence is not in a trusting mode right now for any woman. He sounds tough sometimes and he looks tough, but he's a real teddy bear underneath. At least, he was when we first got to know him and until Darla. Darla . . . somehow, that changed him."

"He must have loved her very much. He must still love her." Cary averted her eyes. She was surprised herself at the ache the realization brought. She felt as if she'd been rolled over by one of those giant bulldozers she'd dreamed of. And she had to face the reality that for Spence she was a convenient plaything, someone to snarl at, someone to snap at, someone to grab in anger. Mary must have sensed the stream of emotions flowing over Cary.

"Are you okay?" In the firelight, it seemed that Cary had actually paled and now her face flamed.

"Darla called for Spence the other night," she said. She was angry at herself for even being physically attracted to such a—such a clod! He was still in love with this sultry Darla who apparently now wanted him back. They'd probably found each other by now. Darla was likely lurking at the funeral to comfort and console him in the loss of his friend.

"Really?" To Cary's ears, Mary didn't sound very surprised, but she reached over and touched Cary's arm, before continuing. "Spence will have to tell you about Darla, Cary. I never liked her, but her leaving hit him hard. Spence and I understand each other. He didn't ask a lot of questions about Jon, and I didn't ask a lot about Darla."

"Jon?" Cary was startled. A Jon had made the pottery she'd admired that first night at Spence's; it had never occurred to her to connect him with Mary.

"Johnny's dad." Mary stretched comfortably on the sofa. "Jon was and is the perpetual restless guy. You're too young to remember that song from the sixties." She sang softly, "And I born to wander and . . . . and I was born the next of kin, the next of kin to the wayward wind." She gazed into the fire. "Jon comes and goes, but for years lately he's been mostly gone. Johnny and I learned not to depend on him. When he comes—if he comes, he's welcome and if we don't hear from him every year or so, we worry. I've made my peace with it. Easy," she smiled at Cary, "to do when the passion's gone."

"And Johnny?"

"We made Johnny legal, and then we—a few years ago—

made ourselves unlegal. Jon's not much for conventional behavior, so it was harder in a way to get us divorced than to get us married! He just doesn't settle down for paper work. Brilliant man, though."

Mary smiled a little. "Jon was never around long enough for Johnny to get totally attached to him. Johnny treats him like any older friend. They've always been honest with each other."

Cary said nothing, absorbing this information. Mary raised her eyebrows. "You're surely not shocked?"

"Oh, no," Cary gave her a hug. "No, but it's certainly different from the Barrymore attitude. I missed all that freedom bit. Little Miss Prettyfrock, that was me growing up in our small town."

"No rebel times?" Mary laughingly asked.

"Well, not until I was old enough to know better!" Cary got up. "Let me make us a cup of tea." Mary was an excellent listener and Cary told her about Smith and about Lanny. They talked until the nearly midnight.

"Mary, you should have been a counselor!" Cary exclaimed at one point. Somehow she wasn't very surprised to hear Mary admit, "I was, once upon a time, but the problems of all those high school kids! Well, they sent me on the road, along which I polished up my natural fluency with language courses and odd jobs, and then I met Jon."

When both women were alternating between silliness and yawning, Mary brought an afghan and covered the drowsy Cary who murmured, "I'm too sleepy to get up and go to bed."

Over breakfast of omelets and muffins next morning, Cary said, "Mary, I'm going to call a friend of mine and see if she can go to the beach with me for a few days."

"Well, now you've surprised me!" Mary munched a bran muffin. "Spence'll be back in a day or so, surely."

"I know, and . . ." she stopped. And I don't want to be

here if he shows up with Darla in tow, she thought. Yes, I'm avoiding seeing him. Call it cowardly. Call it true.

"And," prompted Mary.

"And I'm wondering if I belong here. Maybe it's the rain or Robert's dying, but I need a change of scenery."

"Running away isn't going to solve anything."

"I'm not running away," Cary said hotly.

"You're not staying here," returned Mary, infuriatingly logical. "What do you call it?"

"Spence doesn't trust me. He thinks I'm somehow in with Phillip and that Phillip was in town to buy, to buy ThymeTable."

"To buy ThymeTable? ThymeTable's not for sale, there's never been any question of that! Are you sure he said the farm?" Mary pushed her spoon in circles on the table.

"Phillip didn't say anything definite, typical Phillip, but if not ThymeTable, what then?" asked Cary. "I know something's going on!"

"It's this property, more than likely, that he's checking out, Cary. We scrape by barely making the mortgage each month, but none of us have what you'd call a substantial amount of money to fall back on. Maybe we made a mistake years ago in setting up such huge payments, but we didn't have the cash for a big down payment, so it was a trade-off." A tinge of bitterness invaded her calm recital. "We did assume we'd have Jon's part, of course."

"There's no chance of foreclosure? You are making the payments?"

"At the moment. But I've borrowed recently to pay our share. Johnny can't contribute much yet. Alice and Agnes love it here, and they'll hang on, even if they have to live on goat cheese! Frankly, I'm not sure about Justin. He's in debt for his med school, and keeping the property may not be one of his priorities. Being fair, I suppose I can see why it wouldn't be."

Cary's thoughts were swirling. Yes, the thirty acres of the Cove would be ideal for a development, right up Phillip's alley. But he wouldn't stop there. He'd want more land and better access. He'd undoubtedly want ThymeTable.

Before Cary could say anything, Mary went on, "Of course, if he had some interest to keep him coming back." She looked pointedly at Cary. "He spent a lot of time with you before he left for the funeral."

"Oh, my goodness, Mary! Justin has become a friend, nothing more." She pushed back her chair abruptly and stood. Yes, Justin was strikingly handsome and he had been attentive. But his presence didn't send shocks through her body and put stars in her eyes. Damn Spence. She didn't intend to be on the premises when he returned.

"I'll be in touch before I leave," she promised Mary. "And thanks for listening last night. And for putting me up on your sofa."

"Anytime." Mary hugged her. "I'm here whenever you need me."

Cary called Denise, her college roommate. She operated a small jewelry store that specialized in selling her own beautiful designs. Thus she could travel anytime she wanted to leave the shop in the hands of her capable assistant. They made arrangements to meet at the beach, at Suntip, in two days for a long weekend. Denise had invested in a timeshare there and while she was trying to sell it, she hadn't found a buyer. Periodically she went down to Suntip, to as she put it, "build a fire under the realtor."

"You don't have any eligible bachelors hanging around who'd like to sun and fun for awhile, do you?" Denise inquired, with her contagious giggle. "My last guy was a real bummer. I'll tell you all about it. Men!" Denise was a petite redhead with a temperament that blazed and cooled with amazing rapidity. So far, her record for keeping a steady boyfriend was six months, but she never had any difficulty finding a replacement. Her tales of her relationships were legendary among her friends.

Cary's bag was packed and her car was shining. Johnny had given it a wax job that he said he reserved for Suzanne's car and for his mother's old station wagon. Just as she was locking the door, the telephone rang. Her heart lurched. Spence? She yanked it up, with a breathy, "Hello."

"Cary, it's Justin. Hi."

She sat down, disappointed. "Hello. You caught me just as I was leaving, Justin. Everything okay?"

"Sure. I'm back at work, before seven in the morning til nine at night," he stated. "A martyr but the money's good when the hours are long. Going into town?"

"Actually, I'm off to Suntip Beach with a girlfriend, for a few days."

"Nothing exciting there, huh?" Justin asked. "It is kind of lonesome out there for a pretty girl like you."

"I'm not lonesome, but there's nothing to keep me."

Justin must have misunderstood. His voice took on a flirty sexy tone. "I could join you at the beach."

"No, I—" started Cary.

"The partners have told me to take a day or two. They can't afford to have their busiest young medic totally worn out. I'm not kidding," Justin said. "Give me the address and I'll join you."

Cary didn't want to argue. Even in his persistence, Justin sounded tired and he did deserve a break after his father's death.

"Come on, Cary," he said, "Surely you won't deny a friend who cares about you. I could use some sun and some good company."

He was playing on her sympathy, but so what? What harm could it do. And hadn't Denise practically asked her to bring a man?

"Well, okay." Cary pumped some enthusiasm into her tone as she gave him the address and said goodby.

Suntip was just as Cary remembered it, except perhaps a little less manicured as if the management company were skimping on the upkeep. Denise bounded down the steps to meet her, red hair waving. As they lugged in Cary's suit-cases, she said, "The place needed airing, but it's clean and everything's working!"

She was already far into her story of her latest boyfriend when Cary laughingly interrupted, "Look, I've got to tell you this before he gets here. We'll have company." She gave an abbreviated account of Justin's call.

Denise was delighted. "My only concern," she giggled, "is that I want to finish this tale before Mr. blond god Justin gets here! You won't believe what Alan did after that recep-tion." And she continued her saga of Alan the Terrible. To Cary, it appeared that poor Alan simply couldn't cope with the moods of Denise and the demands of her business. "I really thought he was THE one, Cary," Denise finished dra-matically. Since their sophomore year, they had always re-ferred to their involvements in capital letters.

Cary assured her. "You'll know it when THE one appears."

"Speaking from experience, I dare say," quipped Denise. "Is this Justin THE one?"

A knock interrupted them, and Justin appeared in the doorway, his suitcase in one hand and a bottle of champagne in the other. Handsome in tan pleated pants, his conserva-tively striped shirt called more attention to his features. His hair belonged to the beach scene. Suddenly and cattily Cary wondered if he bought any drugstore help for that too-per-fect blondness. She jumped up to welcome him. Denise's appraising eyes instantly lighted up with approval and com-petitiveness. Unless she were warned off with a baseball bat, Denise considered any man she was introduced to as a po-tential THE one.

Over the long weekend, Justin's presence certainly livened up the condo. He was charming to both and made no clear effort to get Cary alone. Denise flirted as always and asked Cary bluntly when the two of them went for Justin's favorite beer, "Are you interested in him, Cary? If you aren't, then," and she made an expressive face, "the field is wide open. Open season!"

"Oh Denise, you and your hunting! Justin is a friend. And he more or less invited himself." She shrugged. "I don't have any claim on him. Truly."

The three of them took long walks on the beach and short splashings in the ocean. It was too cool for doing much more than quick dips and quicker dryings. They drove up the coast to go dancing at one of the fairly new "Cowboy" nightclubs and they ate out every meal except breakfast. One day at lunch, Cary's mind was elsewhere—back at ThymeTable Farm—and for a few moments she let the conversation wash around her. When the words "Randall family" penetrated her consciousness, she realized Denise was telling Justin about her family and their place in Barrymore society.

"Cary didn't have to worry about money in college," she was saying, "like I did. Now, of course, my business is going great guns and I have more commissions to design than I can keep up with." Cary was both amused and annoyed. Denise was obviously trying to impress Justin with her business sense—but why the discussion of her family?

"I thought you were just a working girl, Cary," he said. "You never mentioned you were rich."

"Rich! Denise, what have you been saying?" Cary was provoked. "I do work. I have worked since college."

They laughed and turned the conversation to something else. I should have been paying attention, Cary thought. Who knows what Denise has said? Probably painted me as the poor little rich girl with the broken heart. Sure enough, as they left the restaurant, Justin said, "And you never told me about your surgery. I am a doctor, you know."

He sounded a little miffed.

"My foot's okay. I hardly even think of it at all." She snatched her arm away as he attempted in a doctorly fashion to assist her at the broken curb. Luckily, they were leaving the next day because Cary's patience seemed to be getting shorter with Denise's cute comments and Justin's overly solicitous behavior. She wondered if this possessiveness on his part was an attempt to make Denise sit up and take notice of him. Of course, she was already doing that. At some point, she had invited him to call her Deni, a sign that Cary recognized as meaning "I'm interested in you and willing to see where this leads."

As they said their goodbyes in the condo parking lot, Cary was eager to get on the road and get back to ThymeTable. Justin kissed her lightly on the cheek, a friendly peck, the twin of which he bestowed on Denise. She and Denise promised to stay in touch, and Justin sent his regards to his father's neighbors. In the little time she'd had uninterrupted and alone, Cary had been acutely aware that two-thirds of her was not at the beach; her body was eating seafood, drinking iced tea and light beer, and sunning in a bright purple bikini, but her mind and heart were in the mountains of western North Carolina. So much, she thought, for all the good it did to get away for a change of scenery. Justin had not noticed her preoccupation, but Denise had gazed at her questioningly a couple of times.

During the long drive back to the farm, Cary concentrated on blankness. She couldn't ignore the current of excitement that passed through her every time she thought of Spence and the power of that current when she saw him, so she willed herself into a state of exclusion. She excluded every thought and paid absolute photographer's attention to the scenery through the Piedmont. A rush of pleasure surged

through her at her first view of the mountains as the Interstate brought her close to Old Fort.

The next morning Cary got up early, had a quick breakfast, and took her camera to the greenhouse to shoot her
basil pot, feeling vaguely guilty that it should have grown a
few days without her attention. She positioned the basil for
the best light, brushed a speck of dust from it, and adjusted
the aperture carefully. Totally engrossed in her work, she
didn't hear Spence come into the greenhouse.

"So you're back."

Cary jumped and almost dropped her camera. Instantly
she turned, her eyes flashing. If she'd fantasized (and perhaps she had, just a little) about their meeting, she had assumed that she would be in control, cool, remote, and that
Spence would beg forgiveness, would do something sweet
and tender. Certainly, his words didn't sound sweet.

"And you're back too!" Decidedly not brilliant, but the
best she could do with her thoughts in disarray.

Apparently Spence hadn't expected to be put on the
defensive. He surveyed the flushed Cary. "Did you enjoy your
beach stay with Justin?"

"Yes, I did!" returned Cary, with more enthusiasm than
truth. "And whose business is it?"

"Not mine you mean?"

"Exactly." Cary repositioned the basil plant. "I've got to
get this picture. If you'll excuse me."

"Leave the damn plant," Spence growled. "What in the
hell did you mean dashing off—"

"Dashing off?" All the confusion of that last night when
he'd so abruptly accused her of not being trustworthy and
then had the audacity to try to kiss her froze her voice.

She said with all the haughtiness she could muster, "You
left, too."

"I had business to attend to," said Spence, studying her.
"And I guess you had business, too. Too bad Robert's death

kept you here a few days. You could have had all sorts of deals accomplished—"

"You're arrogant and you're wrong, Spence Bradford. You couldn't see the truth if it—" Cary faltered just a moment, "if it was growing right in front of your face!"

She turned on her heel, jerked her camera from the table. "And you can keep your precious Darla. You deserve each other. I won't try to compete with her."

Spence's eyes blazed with astonishment and something akin to amusement, but Cary didn't see it. She marched from the greenhouse.

Cary halted at the garden. To calm her beating heart she stooped to pick an herb. She crushed the spearmint between finger and thumb, allowing its fragrance to invade her very senses. Breathing in slowly to savor its essence, she willed her pulse to slow, her anger to dissipate. I can handle this, she thought, I can deal with his arrogance and suspicion. It was unlike her to lash out so stingingly, to deliberately hurt another's feelings.

Even as she inhaled, eyes closed, trying to control her trembling, she was suddenly aware of his breathing, quiet and very near. Her nostrils flared, her knees were actually shaking. Not since the fourth grade when she'd bumbled so helplessly during the county spelling bee had she felt so weak. Yet the morning sun—or Spence's presence—had brought a flush to her cheeks.

She stood immobile, reluctant to turn, since she had stalked, yes stalked, from the greenhouse. She knew he had advanced toward her but she could not turn. Facing his strong jaw and his eyes, darkened probably by fury would be impossible. The moment was a century. A light brush of lips on her neck, so slight it might have been a Monarch's wings sent her spirit soaring, but reason kept her rooted to the spot. His lips were warm, nudging her hair aside. Her heart pounded violently. His body was now against hers, lightly, making Cary doubly aware of every point of contact. His hands were on her shoulders, moving down her bare arms, now encircled, his palms clasped her elbows gently. His breath near her ear was as still as the forerunner of a whirlwind.

"Hey," he whispered. "My spearmint girl. Hmm. Delicious."

Her every fiber begged her to melt with abandon into his arms; his body gave off a warmth as close, as clean as the earth he tilled so lovingly.

Cary steeled herself inwardly as she said, "I'm sorry I called you arrogant. But you . . . " She could say no more. Her arms ached to hold him but she clung to the camera.

"Yes." He cradled her, his lips light, yet insistent. With fingers roughed by his morning's work and smelling of rosemary he turned her face to him, tilting her chin slightly. His voice husky and low, he muttered, "I'd like you to stay, and more than that." In the desire in his face, she saw too a reluctance at odds with his words. As unlikely a match as the fragrances of rosemary and spearmint that surrounded them, she thought as she met his hungry lips. Then she thought no more.

The kiss began slowly as if, in spite of his words, he were uncertain of her response. When her lips parted under his, her weak hands lowered her camera to the ground and her arms went up to hold him closer and closer, Spence pulled her to him.

Chapter 6

Cary was caught up in the sensuality of the long savoring kiss, a kiss expert, a kiss that promised more, that snared her senses as a dewdrop lingers warm in a sunflower, aware of the precipice. Spence crushed her to his chest where she fit perfectly, her breasts molded against his torso. She hardly breathed before his lips descended again, rougher, tormentingly demanding. Even as she surrendered and swam in the sensation, her brain maintained a tiny bit of distance. A line of poetry from her sophomore lit book flitted across her mind, describing Lancelot and Guinevere's first kiss in a garden as "when both our mouths went wandering in one way."

Maybe the wisp of poetry reminded her that they weren't the lovers of old, that they had recent harsh words to deal with. She snapped back to reality.

"This, this is crazy, Spence," she stammered.

"There's nothing crazy about the way I feel," Spence said. "I feel very sane." He held her more closely, "and very sexy." He turned her face to him and asked wryly, "Are you sure you don't feel anything? You have a certain glow about you. I was sure you felt something!"

Cary touched her tender lips and said resolutely, "I was thinking about Guinevere and Lancelot, if you must know."

"God help me!" Spence exclaimed, releasing her in mock outrage. "I try to make love to you and you're back with the knights of the round table. I see my technique is sadly lacking."

Then he gently lifted her fingers which still held the spearmint and gazed at her steadily, as if he were deep in thought. Cary knew that she must break the spell. "We do need to talk."

Spence dropped her hand as if it held a bumblebee.

"I'm sorry if I took undue advantage of you just now, Cary. You were so angry at me and so beautiful that I overstepped the limits of a landlord." His voice was flat, as if he were speaking to some catalog clerk in a mail-order business.

"I guess," he said slowly, his dark eyes surveying her with measured deliberation. "Justin has more claim than I do. The beach obviously agreed with you. Is doctor Justin back at work, making medicine and money?"

Her pulse still pounding from Spence's kisses, Cary had a hard time making the transition from the physicality of Spence to his inane remarks about Justin.

"What are you talking about, Spence? What claim?"

"Cary, I swear, sometimes I don't think we're ever on the same wave length. I'm wondering if I should congratulate you on hooking the eligible doctor." He turned away.

Cary looked at him with exasperation. He walked toward Rosemary whistling some mournful tune. This man is driving me to distraction, Cary thought, trailing behind him. We quarrel, we kiss, then we talk about Justin! Just as they reached the steps of the cottage, the telephone shrilled.

"Let it ring," Spence growled, throwing his body on the steps. Exactly what Cary was thinking. Perversely, though, the moment Spence commanded her to ignore it, she increased her speed and reached the phone on the sixth or seventh ring.

"Hi, it's me, Denise." Before Cary could do more than say hello, her friend bubbled on. "The beach was great, wasn't it? I just called to see how you're doing."

Cary knew that Denise was trying to gauge her friend's feelings toward Justin. If Cary "claimed" him, Denise, no matter how predatory her instincts, would back off, at least for the time being.

"I'm fine. It was a long drive, but I slept late. I'm glad to be back home, back to the cottage though." She had called Rosemary Cottage home without thinking, remembering the rush of pleasure and satisfaction when she pulled into the drive.

"That Justin is some kind of hunk, Cary. I love that blond hair! Gorgeous, don't you think?"

Cary laughed. "He is some kind of hunk! Unattached too."

"If you're okay with it," Denise announced candidly, "I'm going to invite him over to the studio soon. There's a big crafters' convention at Roanoke in a couple of weeks and I could use an escort."

"Could you be looking for a new THE one?" teased Cary.

Keeping her eyes on the sprawled figure of her landlord, Cary fidgeted impatiently. She was afraid Spence would leave his comfortable lounging on the steps. He reached up carelessly and ran his hand through his brown wavy hair. That gesture sent her blood racing again. She wanted to run her fingers through his hair, to pull his face to hers, to taste his lips, to feel that faint stubble roughness. When Denise said goodby, Cary almost slammed the phone down in her eagerness to join Spence. Inexplicably she turned shy and stood immobile near him, wondering what next.

"You wanted to talk, Cary. Here I am. Talk."

A dozen questions flashed through Cary's mind: do you trust me, where were you, who's Darla, what does she mean to you? She blurted out, "Are you going to sell ThymeTable?"

"You know anybody interested in buying?" asked Spence with unwarranted callousness.

"Believe me or not, Spence," Cary spoke quietly, "I did not know why Phillip and Alecia came to Asheville. What I know now is mostly by guessing." The moment the thought entered her head, Cary asked with vehemence, "And how do I know those kisses weren't some kind of ambush!"

"Come on now," Spence declared. "You surely wouldn't have enjoyed an ambush."

She blushed. "I might if I'm ambushed by a master."

Spence merely put his chin on his fists and raised his eyebrows, regarding her as if she were a persistent pre-schooler. And under his scrutiny, that's the way she felt.

"That good, huh?"

"Oh," Cary was at a loss for words. She wasn't about to admit that yes, he was that good, and that she wanted to sit beside him, take his tousled head in her arms and cover his face with kisses. Willing her voice into a light taunting tone, she quoted, "As the plowboy poet once put it: O wad some Power the giftie gie us to see oursels as ithers see us!"

"It would from many a blunder free us and foolish no-tion," Spence finished. "Right."

"Were you an English major?"

"Not I," Spence admitted. "My mother was, so I have a few lines stored up. So, just how should I see you, Cary? Since you see me as an ambusher, are you a neat little sneak?" He held up his hand. "You arrive at ThymeTable when admittedly I'm at a low point and the others are in financial—well, they're in an uncertain time. Not a week later, Phillip Randall of R&R Developers is in town, dining with the Pullmans and God knows who else. Just passing through? No ulterior motives? Just visiting his baby sister?"

Cary stared horror-stricken at his recital, dismayed and angry, yet understanding rationally how he could draw his conclusions.

"Spence, let me explain,"she began.

"No, let me get all this out. I'm not too worried about ThymeTable Farm. With a lot of work and the rest of my savings—what Darla didn't take—I can make a go of this place. If I decide to stay."

"If you decide to stay? Aren't you sure? Aren't you committed to the farm?"

"You don't know me very well, Cary. Do you think I grew up here? That I'm tied here by family history?"

In the fractional pause before he went on, Cary realized that he didn't know that Mary had told her anything. She also realized that in fact she did know very little about him.

"My family aren't into farming, herbal or otherwise. They're business and my degree is strictly business, MBA, Wharton. Right after college I joined the Peace Corps for a stint in Senegal." He fingered the medallion at his neck. "I wasn't ready to settle down right then to a nine-to-five job or to one woman, for that matter. So, as Mary puts it, I dashed off to the safety of foreign shores." His darkened eyes seemed to be seeing those shores.

"It wasn't a picnic, believe me. I almost died a couple of times." At her quick look of concern, he smiled a little. "Nothing romantic. No bullet or saber wounds. Just plain sickness. Stomach infections. Pneumonia. Out in the villages, we were pretty far, days in fact, from the kind of medicine and treatment I needed. Anyway, when I got to a hospital finally, there was a girl there, a Brit, volunteer nurse. She gave me this." He indicated the necklace. "I realize now that I loved her for saving my life and I keep this as a reminder of her. She, well, she almost fell in love with me, but when her doctor boyfriend came out, she made her choice and I recovered, actually sooner in spirit than in body."

Spence stared at the neckpiece with a bemused look. "I needed her and she nursed me through that bad time, but she knew you don't base a marriage on need. Besides," he grinned, "I was a physical wreck, not the prime specimen you see before you today!"

"Go on," Cary urged. "You must have been very young then. Oops! Sorry about that."

"Pretty young. I was ready to go to graduate school when I returned from Senegal. Getting the degree was a breeze partly because I so thoroughly enjoyed the pleasures of my bachelor apartment and all the conveniences I'll never take for granted again. And since I didn't have any burning plans to save the world for awhile, it was easy enough to go into the savings and loan work."

Cary seated herself a few feet away, on a lower step. Banking? This lean blue-jeaned, booted herb farmer ensconced behind a desk, polished to a sheen, no doubt, with a name plate and a stack of forms in front of him? She'd grown up with business types. She'd assumed she could recognize them in an instant. "Savings and loan?"

For an instant Spence's bitterness turned his eyes dark and stoney. "Savings and loan. And I was one of the scapegoats when they started on that swift fall. No, I didn't do anything illegal, but that's beside the point. If I had been a couple of notches further up the ladder, it would have been my head that fell. As it was, it was my job and . . ."

"And," prompted Cary.

"And my belief in the business, I guess. I'd gone into it without much thought, just because it was there. Family, you know. And it didn't provide much challenge. I was sliding along, wondering what to do—really do—that is, when I wasn't working or partying. I'm not making excuses, believe me. Maybe I would have gone on up the ladder, given the money and all it can provide; maybe I would have gotten out on my own, given my growing dissatisfaction. Maybe I was lucky that the choice was made for me. Anyway, down it went and out I went."

Now Cary's eyes surveyed him, sweeping from his broad

forehead, down his chest, his long legs, to his feet. She remembered Spence in his well-cut suit, his perfectly matching tie, his polished shoes.

"But, but, from that kind of job, that kind of life, to this, to ThymeTable?"

"An old friend of mine, of the family actually, had come out here and tried to live the good life, to be as self sufficient as possible. He didn't even like the encroachments of paved roads close by, so when he wanted to move on, to Alaska, he contacted me. I bought the place on a lark, but before long I became committed to both enjoying the land and making a living from it. Back in my memory, there was a grandmother with an herb garden and the smell of lavender when I sat on her lap. And, to make a long story short, Cary, here I am."

"And here I stay," Cary murmured.

"And here I stay." Spence repeated. "Now just why I told you all that, I'm not sure. Except you were determined to talk." His voice hardened just a fraction. "And to let you know that ThymeTable isn't going to be a victim for Phillip and his R&R Development plans."

"You do love it, don't you? The planting, the transplanting, the growing . . ."

"I like working with my hands." Spence held out his hands reflectively. "And I like the orderliness combined with the absolute uncertainty of it all. It's an enigma to me. My family doesn't understand it although we're only a couple of generations removed from a Midwestern farm. But they accept it. Especially since the savings and loan bust was a sort of done deal. I guess they're glad I came out clean—well, clean, but a little tarnished, at least emotionally. Frankly I'm happy to be fighting a different kind of battle. Me and the elements. And I had it pretty much together." He stopped abruptly, and then went on, "How about a cup of morning tea? I hear you've been brewing and stewing, a regular little homemaker. Care to prove it?"

More than tea Cary wanted to know what he would have said next, after the "had it . . . together." Where had Darla come in and what had her leaving done to Spence? But she jumped up with a military salute.

"Tea coming right up."

They were seated comfortably in Rosemary a few minutes later with a steeping teapot before them and a plate of Mrs. Alison's thickly-sliced oatmeal molasses bread.

"I mixed up some cream cheese along with some thyme and dried tarragon for the sandwiches," Cary said. "We should wait a few minutes for the flavors to mix. But suddenly I am very hungry." She began to devour the crusty sliced bread. "Hmmm. Okay, but it will be even better later."

Spence sipped his tea appreciatively. Cary broke the silence to ask about Robert's funeral , which now seemed such a long time ago, and about which Justin had said nothing. They talked about Robert, his courtliness, his love of rare old books.

"I'm sorry I wasn't here when he died. I was in Mexico, actually back in Texas when I called Mary to tell her the news . . . and learned about his attack."

"The news?"

"I went down to Mexico City, near there, to find Jon. It took a while."

"To find Jon?" Cary repeated. "I sound like your personal echo. But why did you, I mean, what's Jon got to do with Robert or with anything?"

"Jon signed on to help Mary with their share of the Cove's payments. But he forgets. He simply moves on and loses track of promises he's made." Spence wiped his fingers on his jeans, ignoring the petite luncheon napkin Cary had placed near his cup.

"Mary's been hurting lately for money, and she's too proud to accept a loan from me. If they're really desperate, she would, but meanwhile, I wanted Jon to know just where they stood. We're good friends and I'd trust him with my life. But, as I said, he tends to move on. Anyway, he's doing quite well. Hooked up with an import-export firm on the side and potting for fun."

Cary thought he deliberately finished the sandwich slowly just to tease her curiosity. "Well, what happened?" she demanded.

"Well, little miss nosey," Spence said, "we had fun in the sun and the bars. And I laid it out for him. Mary and Johnny needed some help. Jon is anything but stingy. Money just doesn't mean much to him. He came through with enough for the moment and a promise of more. It wouldn't surprise me if he shows up here sometime soon." Spence grinned crookedly. "I enjoyed Mexico. We'll have to go there sometime."

"Sure," Cary said sarcastically. "I'm in the habit of rushing off at the slightest invitation—"

"You seem to be," Spence challenged her. "Didn't you just return from a quick weekend at the beach!"

"That was uncalled for," Cary declared. "And besides, I invited—"

"You invited Justin," Spence drawled. "Well, then, why can't I invite you?"

Cary gazed at the self-satisfied smirk on Spence's face. A devilish urge to wipe that smirk off his face may have prompted her action. She didn't intend to analyze it.

Stretching sexily, she slowly rose from her chair and went over to the sofa. She sat down next to Spence, her thigh matching his, and she sensuously twisted her body so that her breasts touched his shirtfront. She ran the fingers of her right hand down his chest in a tantalizingly slow movement while her left hand went around his neck.

With her lips brushing his cheek, Cary sighed what she hoped was a lover's sigh although she suddenly wondered if this joke on him was turning into a joke on her. Her breath was more ragged than she planned and her heart pounded wildly, so that she drew back just a fraction. "If you mean it, Spence," she breathed, "just say when. I'm free to accept invitations." The words of a country song cliche came to mind, as she twined her fingers through his hair at the collar. She murmured, "Free, but not cheap."

Spence sat as if in a trance. When she turned her body against his, his hands had automatically started to grasp her waist, but he had dropped them quickly. "Damn, Cary! What are you doing?" He pushed her away abruptly and stood up, his chest heaving. "Not cheap! You little, you little . . . . " He clamped his lips shut when he saw Cary's face. She burst into laughter.

"That'll teach you, Spence!" She giggled. He looked as dumbfounded at her behavior as if he'd just witnessed a favorite niece propositioning a stranger. Cary was half lying on the sofa where she'd slipped when Spence stood up. Glad the pillow covered her face, she willed her racing pulse to slow to normal. Her playacting had ended when she laced her fingers through Spence's hair. Had he not broken the embrace, she would have kissed him with a passion that might have amazed him.

Spence had the good grace to also laugh, but it was a little strained. He glowered. "Testing me, huh?"

"No, teaching you not to throw out invitations like that. Cheap invitations!" Cary went into another spasm of laughter.

"Lesson learned, madame schoolteacher," Spence said ruefully. He stood with his hands on his hips as she began to gather the tea things. "You're always surprising me, Cary."

Spence took the tray before she could stop him. He set it down in the kitchen and turned to Cary. "Now, let me teach you something."

He pinned her close, so close she could hardly breathe and while she squirmed to free herself his lips traced patterns down a cheek, up, over her nose, on her eyelids. She stopped

squirming as his mouth covered hers in masterful posses-
sion. The emotions she had not succeeded in quelling when
she was teasing him surged over her. Cary pressed harder
against Spence, wanting to merge her body with his as their
mouths were merged. It was a long kiss, prolonged as his
tongue tasted her lips insistently yet lazily and then moved
from her lips downward to the hollow of her throat. Cary
moaned slightly and her arms around his back invited him to
continue. With a kiss at the first button of her blouse, a running of his tongue over her flesh, Spence wrenched away.
Cary, limp with desire, stumbled and clutched the cabinet
behind her.

"That's lesson number two," Spence declared. "I learn
very quickly." In an instant he was gone.

Cary ran a glass of water from the faucet and drank deeply.
True, Spence was no slow learner. And neither was she. She
had never felt such longing, such sexual desire, and she
would have welcomed Spence's lovemaking here in the
kitchen, anywhere. She wanted him completely. She drank
more water. And she didn't want to play games where she'd
be hurt. No more. She declared to herself. He's off limits.
She realized that once again she had learned nothing about
the elusive Darla. Nor had she told Spence that Darla had
called. In fact, she hadn't learned anything about his current
situation—love situation, that is. She stood in thought for a
long time, digesting what Spence had told her of himself,
running it all through her mind again until she came to the
"lesson" at the end. Chagrined and chastened, she renewed
her determination to leave the man alone. He was Darla's
and probably happy about it. He had likely visited her or she
had tracked him down. He surely hadn't been in Mexico all
those days?

Cary grabbed her camera and drove into town to the
safety of the photography studio.

Chapter 7

The shaft of late morning sunlight entered the window and hit the table's display perfectly. Over the past few days while having her coffee Cary had paid close attention to that slant of light. She had even timed it so today she had her camera ready. She was proud of her morning's work.

The scent of cucumber soup lightly garnished with dill would almost permeate the photograph, she thought. In a large half of a green pepper artfully cut she had poured the chilled soup, carefully arranging the dollop of yogurt and the sprig of dill atop it and placing the yeast rolls with the light butter glaze to the side. A yellow-eyed pansy completed the plate, itself a burnished ebony, a lucky yard sale find.

Cary crouched at the table edge, positioning herself close to the arrangement, deftly touching the items until they were arrayed to her satisfaction. She snapped half a dozen shots, moving to try different angles. She was confident that this entry into the gourmet magazine's "Food Fresh from the Garden" contest had a good chance of winning in the amateur division. She'd tasted, tried, re-tasted, revised the soup until she never wanted to see a cucumber again. Brushing her hair back with a satisfied smile, she put the camera aside and sat down to taste her now fully photographed concoction.

"You're devouring your model?" asked Spence.

How long, Cary wondered, had he been standing there, just outside the door? He came in when she looked up. It would be churlish to bite into the roll without offering him lunch. She gestured casually toward the refrigerator. "There's more soup, but I've used the last of the yogurt. Help yourself."

Spence poured his soup into a large soup bowl he'd rummaged around in the cabinet to find, and he did not ignore the garnish. A true herb man. He pinched the dill to release its pungent odor, sprinkled it liberally on the soup, helped himself to a couple of rolls, and sat down across from her.

"Your arrangement is quite fetching," he commented. "Any reason for the photo session?"

Cary had not told him of the contest nor of her constant revising of the soup recipe their cook Jemmie used to prepare for an occasional luncheon of her mother's friends. If she won—and it would be weeks before she'd know—it would be her surprise.

"Just practicing and enjoying my Saturday morning soup-making."

"You're up to something," Spence said. "And this something is good."

A warmth spread through Cary at his words. After all she wasn't completely sure of her own taste buds, especially when she was trying to capture her creation on camera.

Spence ate with the gusto of a man who has been up early and worked for several hours, and who also appreciated good food. He spread butter on the second roll, looking totally relaxed at her table. The sunlight now slanted off his jaw, already faintly darkened. Cary wanted to photograph his face; she wanted to reach over and lightly brush his arm, to stroke its brown hair.

Could making soup cause you to feel so tenderly and motherly toward anyone, especially your landlord, who was enjoying your final product so thoroughly? wondered Cary. Candidly, she had to admit that what she was feeling toward Spence at the moment was anything but motherly. Cary and Spence had—without words—put into effect a truce following their last encounter. He treated Cary with the courtesy of a distant cousin, sometimes stopping for a brief chat, especially if he were going into town. And Cary responded in kind.

This unexpected visit was the first time since Cary's "sofa game" that he had sat down. His presence brought all her senses to alert and Cary simply liked having him across the table, even so nonchalantly wiping his mouth in satisfaction. On the other hand, how could he be so casual, acting as if they'd never kissed, never quarreled, never touched. It wasn't as if he were at a restaurant and she a waitress sitting opposite. Cary's fiery cheeks reflected her internal monologue. Ready to make a caustic comment, she turned to Spence.

"How's Justin?" Spence asked.

"Fine, I suppose. And busy."

"I'm sure he'll find some time to come down to see about the house," Spence said, "if nothing else."

Fishing, Cary thought, with some amusement, Spence is fishing for information. Well, she didn't know any more than he did about Justin's plans.

"I suppose," murmured Cary. She gazed out the window at the two cardinals nearby. They often put in an appearance near the lunch hour and she watched their darting from branch to branch with interest. She also waited to see what else Spence might say because she sensed a tension, a waiting.

"Seen your brother yet?"

"What?" Cary jerked her head back in total surprise.

"Phillip is in town, surely you knew," he said drily. "And I don't suppose you've seen the paper either." He pulled a folded local daily paper from his back pocket and tossed it on the table between them.

"Interesting article on page three." He watched the cardinals flit through the yard.

Cary snatched the paper and opened it. The short article in the business section announced: New Golf Complex Proposed. The headline, however, was more definite than the actual news item itself. It indicated that Phillip Randall of the well-known Virginia firm of R&R Developers was meeting with prominent local businessmen and town officials. Cary couldn't believe what she was reading. "Negotiations are underway" the article said, to purchase a large tract of land outside the city limits, in the western section of the county. More details would be forthcoming within a few weeks as negotiations continued. Phillip Randall preferred "no further comment" until the details were finalized. Local authorities looked forward to working with R&R Developers.

Cary's stomach felt as if Alice and Agnes' goats were trampling through it in a mad rush to their favorite carrots. She exhaled raggedly and pushed the paper back across the table. She'd heard nothing from her brother and Alecia. Yet she wasn't completely shocked.

Niggling in the back of her mind had been the fear that Phillip was working his deals. That is what he did, the way he made his living, his business. She would prefer no development, certainly none of the sort that changed Suntip Beach, but if there had to be some, then why here? Sheer coincidence? Thoughts swirled around in her head like the mix in a milkshake blender, thoughts she had refused to entertain earlier. Had she brought Phillip here? Was she responsible? Would Phillip be negotiating had she not left Barrymore for

Asheville? Spence simply waited, a wary look neither condemning or absolving, just waiting.

I feel a nameless sadness o'er me roll, thought Cary. She wanted to put her head down on the table like a weary child. She had to say something but what could she say that would erase the implacable blankness from Spence's face?

"I had nothing to do with it," she stated as if she were on the witness stand. "And I'm terribly sorry." Her tone took on a defiant note, "You have made up your mind and no matter what I say, you won't believe me at all!"

Spence retrieved his paper and tucked it in his back pocket. As if he were measuring each syllable, he said, "I think the lady does protest . . . too much?"

"That's what I mean! You'll believe what you want."

"And you know what I want to believe?" he asked.

"You want me to be guilty of betraying you, don't you?" Cary blurted, astonished at her words. "You want me to be another Darla!"

"Now that is an interesting twist, dear Cary. Aren't you trying desperately to change the subject? What's Darla got to do with all this?" Spence raked her with his eyes. He scowled, "You are hardly in Darla's league."

Cary's eyes smarted. I will not cry, damn it, she thought. Not in Darla's league. Not beautiful, not alluring, not appealing, not sensual. Nothing that Lanny had ever said hurt as much as Spence's casual declaration.

Spence gazed out the window, his mouth a bitter line. "Surely, you can see that any of us, Johnny, Mary, could wonder at the connection—the coincidence, if you will. You arrive one day and R&R arrives very soon thereafter. No," he said, when Cary gripped the table's edge, "they haven't said anything. Very trusting. You may have fooled them, Cary. But me? I wish you hadn't tried to fool me."

"I didn't."

"You weren't Phillip's advance guard?"

"No!" Cary raised her voice. "That's not why I came out here."

"Oh?"

Very quietly Cary began to speak. "I left an abusive relationship in Barrymore, one I'm not proud of and one I can't quite explain either to myself or to anyone else. Certainly not to you."

Cary looked outside. The cardinals had left the yard, but she studied the pleasant landscape as if it were a vacant canvas and she were creating a masterpiece upon it, thinking, in fact, that she would plant it in her memory so that when she left she could take it with her. For leave she must. She couldn't stay near Spence who didn't trust her, didn't want her around. And at the thought of the Cove or ThymeTable being developed, Cary shuddered.

"What do you mean?" Spence asked.

"What does it matter? I mean abusive, the nice sanitized word for hurting someone, verbally mostly, and, and more." Her voice quavered slightly. "I don't intend to discuss it."

Spence was on his feet instantly. He came around the table and took her arm. Perhaps his grip was stronger than he intended. Cary burst into tears. "Don't touch me!"

Spence dropped his hand, looking helpless. Cary started into the living room. "Just go, Spence." She wiped her cheeks and murmured somewhat sardonically, "As King Lear said in another context, 'Weep, no I'll not weep.'"

Realizing Spence stood just behind her, Cary said again, "I meant it. Landlord you may be, but if I'm going to cry, I prefer to do it in private."

"Cary, I don't intend to leave. You're distraught. Come here." Spence pointed to the sofa. "Sit down. I don't want to pry, but I think you could tell me about it." He dragged a handkerchief from another back pocket and handed it to her.

"Who knew men still had a handkerchief ready?" she gulped. "Your pockets are full of surprises."

"I'm listening if you want to talk, Cary. As a friend." He sat beside her and put an arm around her shoulders, very much as her father would have done.

"There's not much to tell," Cary began, but she found within the comfort of his arm, there was a great deal she needed to say. She told him about Lanny and her fall. She told him about her family, their house, and community. Spence himself spoke hardly at all; he kept his arm around her and she rested her face on his chest occasionally and he encouraged her to continue with a slight squeeze or a simple question when she faltered.

"Dumb of me to run off, I guess, to retreat," she ended. "It's been nice, though." She gave a little laugh, her eyes now dry, and only a slightly red nose as a reminder of her tears. "I needed that!"

"Sometimes somebody outside your family can hear you differently. I know I was glad to have somebody in Senegal. Feel better now?"

"Yes. Thanks for listening. You said you provided all kinds of services, but I never expected to call on you for therapy sessions."

Spence matched her light tone. "Glad to be of assistance, ma'am."

Cary's head was no longer on his chest, and now he took his arm from her shoulders. " I'd better be going. There's a lot to be done before the Fair next week."

"Let me help you," offered Cary.

"No, no. I'll manage." Spence seemed a little uncertain. "I need some time in the greenhouse." The sentence ended with something unspoken, and Cary supplied it mentally, "Alone." He had been kind, he had listened to her outpouring, but he still had to deal with the reality of the newspaper article. He might be a kind and wonderful listener, but his farm or his neighbors' place was at stake.

Cary took a deep breath. "Spence, I can't stay here under

this shadow. You don't trust me or my family. I'll pack up and be gone in a couple of days."

Spence froze in his walk toward the back door. Then he faced her squarely. "Don't be a fool, Cary. You belong here. This trust thing is something I have to work out." He flung open the screen door. "Stay and face it. Try that route!"

Cary sank limply into a chair. She kept her eyes on his back as he walked away, the newspaper in his back pocket showing like a flag of battle. He was daring her to stick it out, to not run away. Of all the nerve, she thought, when Mary had told her it was Spence's way of solving too many quandaries. He had the gall to dare her to stay and face whatever the consequences. What did he mean, you belong here. Yes, this seemed more like home than her apartment among the students, but she couldn't stay when obviously he still thought she was connected with Phillip's deal.

She was thankful that he had not said more, not been more physical. His warm arm around her had not been intrusive. He had allowed her to see her responsibility for staying with Lanny, had not tried to place all the "blame" on Lanny. Her parents had been perhaps too kind and she had snuggled up in the warm fuzziness of their concern without coming to grips with herself. Phillip had expected only that she follow his advice, and so she had retreated further into the cocoon of non-responsibility.

Now, what about Spence? They always seemed at cross-purposes. His kisses thrilled her; his presence excited her. Was Darla lingering in his mind. Face it, Cary told herself, you are falling in love with this herb farmer, this businessman and landlord; and that is something you cannot afford to do. He may kiss and he may comfort, but he's someone else's lover even if undeniable magnetic current travels directly from his body to yours. Get out, her rational self counseled, before you get hurt, before you make a fool of yourself.

Regardless of the development mess, don't mess with your heart.

When Cary went into Asheville the following day to work with Mark, he invited her to join him, his wife, and some friends at Richmond Hill, Asheville's restored Victorian mansion overlooking the French Broad River. The graciousness of the building required, Cary thought, a certain dressing up and she drove back to Rosemary to change into a suitable party frock. The dinner at Gabrielle's was wonderful and the company delightful. The more people she met in town, the more Cary liked and appreciated Asheville. While her companions toasted her success as a photographer with excellent champagne, Cary smiled gaily. But in her heart she wept at the reality: she would soon be leaving.

Chapter 8

Pictures of the white, fungus-like plant called Indian pipes fascinated Cary. According to her wildflower book, it grew in moist areas. So Cary had awakened with an intense desire to seek out and photograph the strange little plant.

By nine o'clock, walking stick in hand, camera over her shoulder, and a light daypack on her back, Cary had made her way far up the cove. She was heading for the upper reaches of Spring Creek. Several times she had promised herself she would follow the stream as it narrowed farther up the steep slopes of pastureland above the cove. Thus, partly to prevent herself from thinking about leaving and to postpone packing she set out with a mission: to find the strange colorless plant and to go to the very mouth of Spring Creek and perhaps beyond.

Mary had warned her that the climb was strenuous. "You just follow the creek. Going up is not too bad, but coming back puts some strain on those leg muscles!" Mary had grinned lazily. "You'll love it, you with your Wordsworthian bent. It's like the end of the world way up there."

The cows in the pasture raised their heads to watch Cary

stride purposefully along. She skirted around them. She had become accustomed to the side-swagging bovines, but they weren't her favorite animals. She much preferred the lively goats to these passive, staring creatures.

At one point, Cary dropped to the ground to rest, having spread a small piece of plastic to sit on. She had learned in earlier excursions that mountain soil in the early morning could contain a great deal of moisture, and now she always carried plastic in her day pack. She surveyed the long vista before her—only midway up the slope, still in the pasture, although now it was not lush, more scrubby, with clumps of nettles and blackberry briars dotting it.

She had a clear view of the cove and ThymeTable Farm although some of the buildings were hidden by trees and shrubs. She saw the winding blacktop road that neared the Farm and then veered right to circle back toward the French Broad River. The gravel road with its small sign "ThymeTable—2 miles" wound like a piece of grayish rope, following the contour of the land, sometimes lost to her sight as it dipped and curved among slight rises and trees. She wasn't sure, from this distance, just which curve had put her MG into the ditch the day she arrived so inauspiciously.

She remembered her first sight of Spence, slightly sweaty but suave in his work clothes. I should have turned and run right then, she thought ruefully and honestly. I could hardly keep my eyes off his chest, his face, his hands, so what did I do? Fall asleep at his feet practically. She roused from her reverie. Those gentle hands should have warned her: this man is dangerous to any vulnerable woman. And vulnerable she was. But no more, she told herself. He had told her she wasn't in Darla's league and he had held her while she let go of all the grief of Lanny, and he had challenged her to stay—to not run away. The irony was that she must run away from him, not only from his distrust but simply from his body, his presence.

Cary heaved herself from the ground and began walking again. A barbed wire fence, not very tight nor straight marked the edge of the cleared area. The farmer who leased the land had neglected the fence since few animals bothered to wander so far up. She lifted a strand of rusty wire and stooped to step through. The creek here was little more than a muddy trickle.

Cary paused several times just inside the line of trees to photograph the grayed fenceposts, the light filtering through the leaves of the dogwood trees, and to take some long shots of the valley below. For the next few hours she gave herself to the task at hand, absorbed in searching for the Indian pipes and in the meanwhile finding dozens of other mosses, fungi, and minute plants. She checked their identities in her paperback wildflower guide. Many she now recognized from her reading: trailing arbutus, wood violet, bloodroot, false Solomon's seal and starflower.

"Aha!" She discovered the albino plant, growing close to brilliantly colored wild mushrooms. About three or four inches tall, two waxy clusters were emerging, their heads drooped as if in prayer, from a bed of damp leaves. She spent several minutes rigging her flashlight so it would provide sufficient light on the plants after she carefully arranged the piece of black plastic as the backdrop. She was satisfied at last that she had some photographs that would show the little plants in all their delicacy and ghostliness.

She moved away to a sunny spot to drink iced herbal tea from her thermos and to eat a peanut butter and raisin sandwich. Aware suddenly of her fatigue, she glanced at her watch; it was after one o'clock. In the quietness, disturbed only by the aimless twittering of a few birds, she lay back and closed her eyes for a few moments. When she awoke the afternoon was far advanced, and the air was much chillier. Her sunny spot had darkened.

Cary hastened to get her gear together and start back to

Rosemary Cottage. Remembering Mary's comment about sore legs from the descent, she pursued a circular route through the woods, knowing it would take her back ultimately to a seldom used path to the left of the farm. Johnny had once described some interesting rock formations in that direction that he would take her to one day. Since her ThymeTable stay was practically over, she decided to get some pictures of the stones in the afternoon light. The going was rougher than she expected, but she picked her way along carefully.

The jumble of stones, called See-Off by local residents, resembled with some imagination a miniature Stonehenge. Cary scrambled up partway, hesitated, then seeing a foothold, she left her walking stick and hauled herself up one more stone to the top slab that lay at a slight angle.

The view was spectacular and scudding clouds of the late afternoon sent eerie shadows waltzing over the landscape. Cary set her backpack down and began to adjust her camera. She took several shots and then decided to use her zoom lens to survey the scene below. The view included Spence's house and Rosemary Cottage. As Cary zoomed in on the Farm, she brought into focus two figures standing beside a late model burgundy car. One was Spence, and Cary realized instantly that the other must be Darla. The woman was slim, but voluptuous; her flowing ensemble of deep red accentuated her long blond hair. Spence's back was to the camera, but even as a blur, Cary could make out the intensity in the woman's gaze.

Cary's face flamed. She felt as if she had been caught intentionally snooping and had seen the couple in some clandestine situation rather than in the late afternoon outdoors. Spence was holding Darla before him in what was surely a prelude to an embrace. As he grasped her, Darla's face was hidden. Spence moved toward the woman suddenly. He was going to kiss her! Cary couldn't bear it. In a purely reflexive action, she snatched the camera from her eyes and from around her neck.

She breathed deeply, sick at heart. Darla had returned to claim her Spence, and certainly their embrace had seemed imminent. They were kissing at this very moment. Cary sat immobile, visualizing the certainty of the scene she could no longer see clearly. Until that moment she had, perhaps unconsciously, hoped that somehow the elusive and beautiful Darla had rejected Spence once and for all.

Apparently not. Here she was at ThymeTable and in Spence's arms. Cary couldn't bear to put the camera to her eyes again, but she told herself, get it over with. Be sure of what you see. Seeing is believing her mother always said. Feeling like a misplaced spy, she lifted the camera with both curiosity and reluctance. Before she could focus, a noise nearby startled her. A large face poked through the trees, and she dropped the camera in her surprise. It slid down the rock and into a small crevice at the bottom. "Oh, my God," Cary said out loud, horrified. She didn't hear a crash; the camera apparently landed in leaves or soft dirt between the rocks. It probably wasn't broken, but it was certainly out of reach. And, wide eyed, the cow stood chewing her cud, wondering perhaps just what the girl were doing so far up the mountain. Contemplating the fate of her camera momentarily diverted Cary from the two figures far below. Then she shaded her eyes and looked again; she could make them out in a blur. They seemed very close together. Darla was getting into the car. Spence was bent over the door.

Meanwhile, however, Cary surveyed again the hole, some seven or eight feet below into which her expensive camera and lens had fallen. Stupid, stupid, she berated herself. Never, never use a good camera without somehow making sure its strap was attached to you. How many times had her photography instructor emphasized this elementary fact. I cannot go back to Rosemary without it, she thought; the night air might damage it. And then, she'd have to come back up the mountain with Johnny to help retrieve it. She sighed wearily, more tired than she had thought.

There was no easy way down to the camera. If she retraced her way down the rocks to the ground, she could not reach it. It was essentially in the very center of the middle of the formation. The only solution was to inch her way down, inside the formation. Surely she could find some rough spots as toeholds and fingerholds. She had left her walking stick on the ground when she climbed up, but that wouldn't have helped her. It was too short to reach the camera strap. Cary considered her position on the more or less horizontal slab. There was a drop of perhaps four feet and then two or three bulky pillars of stone which were close together formed a kind of vee. Below that in an even narrower slot rested her camera. If she could get to the narrow vee, surely by stretching she could reach the camera.

The sky was rapidly getting darker, and she couldn't waste any time if she was to get back to Rosemary before total darkness. Even with a flashlight she didn't like rambling in the dark through the uneven pasture and the woods.

Cary felt very alone. She couldn't even see the intruding cow. She moved gingerly to the left of where she had been sitting and saw a rougher portion of stone that she could grasp to lower herself. And some shrub had miraculously squeezed part of itself through the rocks. If she could put a foot there, she could lower herself to the vee. She felt fairly confident now that she could figure out how to reach the camera. She looked below for a foothold and placed her hand on the edge of the rock—just as a black snake slithered within two inches of her arm. She instinctively snatched her hand away from the incredibly long form which was moving with startling speed away from her and she suddenly was falling . . . falling.

Cary landed awkwardly, wedged into the vee, her left

foot crumpled under her. Her right hand was scratched and bleeding, two fingernails badly torn. But worse than that and the cut on her forehead was the excruciating pain in her ankle. Her vision blurred and for a moment everything went black. When she opened her eyes again, she wasn't even sure she could sit up, wedged as she was in the narrow opening on her side. Her left arm was under her body, and with the other hand, hurting, she could touch the rock but could not push herself upright.

In another blurry moment, she knew she was close to tears, tears of frustration and some pain. Her foot hurt terribly. Like a sylph in Pope's poem, she was wedged into a bodkin's eye. She grimaced. I am stuck for sure. And where did that damn snake go? She twisted her head as much as possible but she could see no sign of it. Of course, she told herself, it was up on top of the stones, where the sun had warmed the area, and she had disturbed it.

Still, she was hopelessly wedged in among the rocks and who knew what other snakes might be lurking below her or in the other openings in the formation. If I lie here and gather my strength, Cary thought, surely I can at least get turned somehow and sit up. She gritted her teeth as she moved slightly, trying to push up on the arm she lay on. It was no use. I'm stuck. As idle as a painted ship upon a painted ocean. Each move sent unbelievable jabs of pain through her ankle and up her leg. She winced and tears came to her eyes. Her pack with flashlight was a good four or five feet above her—no help. If she yelled no one could possibly hear. Maybe she thought the friendly cow is still nearby. She'd welcome even its face if it could poke it through stone. She was perspiring with the pain even though with the darkness which had fallen so quickly the night was cool.

Just stay calm and wait for a few minutes, she counseled herself, and then you can surely unwedge yourself. What a predicament. Stuck in this little Stonehenge far up where

Spring Creek started. Stonehenge, she thought ruefully, just like Tess in Hardy's novel. I'm getting silly. I have got to get out of here. She tried again to turn her body and in so doing pushed her foot against the rock. This time she cried out in pain and sank back. At least her head was somewhat supported. It was the only part of her body that could be called reasonably comfortable. However, the cut continued to bleed a little.

With her upper arm, she wiped her face, smearing the blood and mingling it with the tears that came unbidden when she moved her leg. For long minutes Cary simply lay, her mind whirling, her ears picking up a tremendous number of night sounds: little scuttlings, twitterings, rustling of leaves, an occasional lowing of a cow far away. She tried not to listen; she didn't want to hear anything that remotely sounded like a slither. She knew black snakes were not poisonous, were not dangerous. Her reaction had been simply instinctive, not actual fear. And she was not afraid now.

She was only hurting and cold. Her wristwatch was on the arm underneath and she could not see the time. After what seemed hours of absolute stillness and silence on her part and all kinds of noises around her, Cary bit her lip and said aloud, "Now, do something. Don't just lie here."

Surely she would be missed. By Mary? Possibly, although she had, stupidly she now reprimanded herself, started out without telling anyone where she was going. Although the two women talked almost daily, Mary might assume she was simply busy. Johnny would likely notice that her light was not on and her car was in the drive. If Johnny chose to come home tonight. Often he stayed in town until very late. Alice and Agnes had surely called her sometime today and in time they would realize that something was wrong. But they might assume she'd gone into Asheville for the day; they could not see her car from their place. And Spence . . . Spence was busy with Darla, probably dining out, looking unspeakably handsome next to the sensuous Darla. Cary didn't want to think about Spence and Darla.

To keep from thinking of her landlord and his lady and to keep her mind off her ankle, Cary began to run through her quotations repertory. She tried to remember every quotation she had ever memorized. She recited the opening lines of the Chaucer's *Canterbury Tales* in a wretched combination of middle English and coastal Virginia sounds. She once decreed (in her sophomoric wisdom) that she could never like anybody who went around quoting Chaucer. One of her sorority sisters had proceeded to "set her up" by bribing a very handsome visiting West Pointer to flirt with her and invite her out. With several sisters nonchalantly close at hand when he came to pick her up, he kissed her hand and began to recite those opening lines. The outburst of giggles from her friends cured Cary at least temporarily from making such vast statements about literature and the male world. The episode was good for giggling sessions for the rest of her college years. Now she wished she could conjure up some of those giggles. The night was very dark. The clouds that had been swirling about earlier had settled like a heavy blanket over any moon and stars that might have kept Cary company.

Stay calm, Cary told herself over and over, like a despairing mantra. When she attempted to raise her body, she could find nothing to grasp with her right hand, her free hand. The more she squirmed, the heavier she felt and the more tightly wedged she became. Finally she exhaled, commanding herself to lie quietly. Someone would certainly search for her and would find her; of that she was confident. She just wished she were as confident of when she would be found. The idea of spending the night in her strained and painful position wasn't pleasant but it was a possibility. She didn't intend to go to sleep because when her rescuers were anywhere near, she wanted to be awake to yell to them. So she continued with her quotations, with a snatch here and there from the early Renaissance. She recited aloud Lovelace's beautiful "Stone walls do not a prison make, nor iron bars a cage," grimacing at the thought of her stone prison. She remembered much of John Donne and was into Milton when she dozed off. She slept for only a few minutes and jolted awake to begin her quotations again. She heard every movement in the trees. The woods seemed amazingly noisy with the slight wind rustling the new leaves. When she awoke again, having dozed while quoting eighteenth century heroic couplets, she realized she must do something else. If Pope's sharp couplets couldn't keep her awake, maybe thinking of her family would.

She thought of her gentle Dad, soft-spoken at home, easygoing on the golf course, mannerly always; but known to be both shrewd and, when necessary, cutthroat in the business world. His colleagues admired his courteous manner and watched his every move, knowing that he took no quarter in battles conducted by boardroom rules although he was an honest opponent. He kept his business out of his household, expecting his wife and daughter to be only nominally aware of finances, and he was a master at turning the conversation to other subjects if they appeared halfway interested. Cary was proud of him, his erect bearing, his patrician features, but she knew that his standard bearer was Phillip.

Phillip, the son of the family, was expected to enter the business and he had shown no rebellion. From his early teens, he had enjoyed going into the firm and he had worked there most summers. He used all the Barrymore contacts in beginning his own business when he was hardly out of college. He'd married a beautiful woman from an old Virginia family and in time they would produce beautiful children. Cary was Phillip's duty, his obligation, and it was only a small step to his believing that her obligation and duty was to be directed by him. Their "clashes" had always been clothed in good manners, and too often, Cary now felt sure, she had given in to Phillip's bossiness in insignificant matters so that he continued to assume his big-brother attitude. She loved him but they were not truly close. She did not open up with him and certainly not with Alecia. Alecia, cool and sophisticated, took Phillip's lead and looked upon Cary as a kind of wayward child. They had been horrified at her involvement with Lanny. And . . . and Spence. Cary replayed the last time they had been together and the other times. He was sensitive and yet he didn't trust her; he was handsome and conceited. Trying to keep his face in her mind and to stay awake so she could hear the rescuers, Cary slept again.

The flashlight's strong beam came from directly above. Cary heard, "My God, there she is!" and she opened her mouth with relief to welcome her rescuer. No words came from her dry throat.

"Over here," Spence yelled. "Johnny, she's over here in these rocks!" The beam played over her body caught in the vee. "Damn, how did she get down there. Are you okay? Cary?" His voice was rough with concern, "Are you okay? Can you speak?"

Weakly, Cary raised her arm in welcome. "I'm okay. Oh, it's good to see you guys." Her words were dry and husky.

"You damn well don't look okay," said Spence, playing the flashlight around, searching for a way down.

He saw Cary's bloodied face, a huge knot on her forehead and he had seen the scratched and bleeding palm when she raised her hand. He scrambled down the rock. He hardly had a few inches to place one booted foot and he propped the other on the stone beside her. He lay the flashlight at her side and tenderly touched her face.

"No, you don't look okay," he said softly. "You look safe and beautiful." His gentle fingers touched her forehead and even though they were light, she sucked in her breath sharply.

"Don't try to move," Spence said. "I'm trying to find out if anything's broken. We've got to get you out of here."

He straightened and yelled again, "Johnny, over here. Down in this damn rock pile."

Johnny yelled back and Cary could hear his footsteps. Another flashlight beam appeared and then Johnny stood above them. "Is she hurt? Cary, you hurt?"

"I'm okay," she said again, managing a grin. "Just kind of sleepy. How can anybody sleep with you guys yelling all over the place?"

"A comic," Spence grunted. He surveyed her body carefully, the flashlight stopping at the ankle, now swollen.

"My lips are dry," Cary murmured. "I'm so thirsty."

"Toss down the thermos, Johnny," commanded Spence. "Careful." Spence caught the object. "I've got it."

He bent closer to Cary and put the thermos to her mouth. She drank the hot chocolate greedily. "Thanks, that was wonderful." Cary heard Johnny strike a match, and she looked up in time to see a flare shooting in an arc through the air.

"Johnny's signaling Mary and the sisters that we've found you. Luckily he had some flares or all of them would be up here with us. That was the only way we could convince them to stay below."

"Can we move her?" asked Johnny. "I could go down and call 911. It'll take them a while to get here."

"Let me finish my examination," Spence said. "We don't want to take a chance, but I think we can get you out of here." He ran his hand down Cary's legs. "No broken bones here. Looks like you twisted that ankle pretty bad." When he touched her foot, Cary muttered an "ouch."

She wasn't sure whether she imagined or heard Spence's muffled "Ah, darling," but she did hear, "Sorry that hurt you."

He considered her position. "I'm going to try to unwedge you. If I can get some leverage here, I can lift you out. Johnny, throw a rope down here, so I can send up this flashlight." He gave Cary another long drink from the thermos and then recapped it and tossed it up to Johnny.

"We can risk losing the thermos, but we need both flashlights to get off this mountain." He was tying the light to the rope when Cary remembered. "My camera. Oh Spence," she faltered, wondering if she should ask more of them.

"What camera?" He followed Cary's gesture at the darkness beneath his feet. "Down there? Is that what got you into this mess?" He turned the beam downward. The camera strap was visible, but in his precarious position, he could not easily maneuver his body any lower.

"Hey, Johnny, cut us a stick, three or four feet long, with a fork at the end. Cary's camera's even farther down in a hole than she is. Maybe I can reach the camera with a stick and pull it up. What did you say, Cary?" Spence had not caught her comment.

She repeated it, and Spence yelled up, "She won't leave here without it!" Johnny laughed and took his light to go find a suitable branch.

"Keep your courage up, kid," Spence said. "We'll have your camera rescued and you too shortly." He didn't like how pale Cary looked in the circle of light and he knew her foot must be terribly painful.

"What time is it?" Cary asked. "I must have dozed off. I quoted all the poetry I could remember, but I kept losing it." She twisted just a little. "I think my watch is broken."

"It's twenty of three." Spence wanted to keep Cary talking. He wondered if she'd cut her wrist. Certainly she was bruised and bloody looking although the cut on her forehead was now dry. He took a handkerchief, wet it with his lips and dabbed at her face.

"How did you know where to look for me?" Cary asked. She too thought she should keep talking. It would be embarrassing to fall asleep with Spence hulking over her.

"Know? We didn't. Sometime around eleven, Mary got worried when you didn't answer. Didn't take long to realize you were gone—on foot. We had a hard time getting Mary to stay put. In fact, we didn't. We spent a good hour checking places close at hand, thinking you might be God knows where, the barns, wherever. Then we set out after convincing Mary to stay put. We did yell for you."

Cary sighed. "Probably when I was sleeping."

"You have a friendly cow at the base of See-Off. It just seemed to be standing there, with its nose turned in this direction. So we came on up. Actually once we got to the head of the creek and the top of the mountain, Johnny said you'd planned on coming up here someday."

"Here you go," Johnny tossed down a thin branch, with a notch on the end.

Holding the light in his left hand, Spence began to fish in the hole, muttering to the camera strap as he manipulated the stick. After several minutes he said, "Here it comes. And here it is." He examined it briefly. "Looks okay, Cary. Here you go, Johnny." He separated the lens from the camera body and carefully threw each to the waiting boy. "Now we're ready to get started on the real rescue. Here comes my flashlight."

Johnny pulled it up and he then positioned both lights so Spence could see clearly.

"Can you manage, Spence. I'd offer to come down, but three's a crowd down there."

Johnny looked around and continued. "I'm going to tie this rope to a couple of trees and you can use it to pull yourself up with."

Spence nodded. He bent over Cary and managed to get his arm behind her head. The other he tried to fit beneath her body but there was simply no space. For a moment he held her head close to his chest. "Cary. Cary. Just don't faint on me. We'll get you out of here."

He lowered her head again to its stone resting place. "Hey, Johnny, throw the rope down here again." Spence smiled encouragingly. "I'm going to tie this rope to your belt loops. You are in here so tight that Johnny'll have to pull you up so I can get my arms under you!"

"Good thing you wore jeans today, Cary," Johnny called to her, obviously trying to keep her spirits up. "What if you'd gone off in sweat pants or something with no loops?"

Cary watched as Spence ran the rope through two belt loops and heaved the end back up to Johnny. "It won't take much to get you up so I can lift you."

"I feel pretty dumb," Cary said. "And that snake made me do it."

"Snake? What kind of snake?"

Spence's frown cleared when Cary muttered, "Black-snake. A big one."

"We can talk about it later," Spence said. "Okay, got yourself anchored up there? We don't want you falling down here and cluttering up Cary's space!"

"I'm ready. Remember, I've pulled lots of cars out of ditches—without a truck. And Cary," Johnny yelled good-naturedly, "you surely don't weigh that much."

He gave a tentative tug on the rope. Spence stood over Cary and said, "Hook your arm over mine to help a little."

It took several tries, with Cary grasping Spence's arm and Johnny tugging on the rope, and then Cary felt her body inch slightly upward. "Just a little more," Spence grunted. "Damn awkward. Sorry if we hurt you, Cary." He was bent almost double as she held his left arm and he slipped the right arm under her body. "Got you," he said.

"I'm heavy," Cary said, woozily.

"Like lead," Spence agreed. He lifted her as gently as possible. "All hundred and fifty pounds of you."

Cary protested, "All hundred and eighteen pounds of me!"

"Whatever," Spence said. "Well, you're unwedged, but getting you out of this rock pile is not over yet. I'm not sure I can climb out and hold on to you. There just isn't any way to get traction."

Cary thought she would be content to remain close to his chest, held firmly. She must have moved in and out of awareness as Spence and Johnny discussed the possibilities of finishing the rescue. She became fully awake when Spence shifted her body slightly and yelled, "Okay, you got it all rigged up? Send it down then."

"We've got a makeshift hoist coming, Cary. Cary, are you awake? Come on, kid," he mimicked Humphrey Bogart. "Don't make this any harder."

"Put me down for awhile, Spence," Cary said. "I can stand on . . ."

"Stand on my foot," Spence returned. "That's all the space there is." He set her down, her good foot on his boot. "Now, let's get this on you."

The hoist was Johnny's heavy canvas jacket. He had constructed a makeshift seat from it and the rope. Spence tied it around Cary's waist and with the ropes and Johnny's belt created a kind of diaper effect. He worked efficiently. At one point, Cary had to cling to him to rest her foot.

"Okay, this will not win a prize for looks, but for sheer ingenuity, this rescue team should win a medal." He sounded cheerful. Johnny, meanwhile, called encouragements and advice. Spence talked to himself as he maneuvered Cary into the sling. "Here we go. I'll just tighten this. Hold on. This has to be shortened. You okay?"

When he was satisfied that Cary was securely tied, he took her face in his hands, hands now rough and looked into her eyes. "You're a brave girl, Cary."

"Woman," she replied faintly, but clearly.

"Huh?" Spence brushed a kiss on her forehead.

"I am woman," Cary said. "You know the song. I am woman."

"Okay, woman. Up you go." Spence picked her up.

"Okay, Johnny. Do your thing. Be careful, though." Spence laughed with relief. "This is woman."

Spence supported Cary as Johnny began pulling on the rope arrangement. Johnny grunted, "And me, tough man." As soon as Cary was beyond his reach, Spence clambered back up the rock to help Johnny bring her over the edge.

"Okay, kid—woman—Cary, you're out of the hole. Now we'll get you home."

Chapter 9

The rest of the night—morning rather—passed Cary by in a kind of whoozy fog. She was slung over Spence's shoulder, if slung were the right word for the careful way he hoisted her from the rock, his arms strong and sure. And she heard him mutter that he regretted the unladylike pose, but carrying her was much easier that way than in his arms. Maintaining his balance on the steep terrain required Spence to keep at least one arm free. With the other he firmly gripped her legs. Her head hung almost at his waist, a position that did not encourage idle banter or chatter. She felt like an ignominious sack of bruised potatoes. Spence had put his jacket on Cary and still she shivered in the chill air.

Descending the mountain, they stopped often to rest. Cary heard the strain in Spence's voice as he tried to keep talking. She couldn't be sure of much that he said. His comments alternated between words of encouragement and apology. "Sorry about that, Cary," he muttered as his foot slipped occasionally. "Still with me?"

"I'm hardly going anywhere," Cary grunted. And in spite of valiant attempts to keep silent, when pains shot through her foot she could not suppress an occasional muffled groan. With youthful dexterity, Johnny led the way, indicating especially rough spots or places where the footing might be more treacherous. Cary in bits and pieces told them about the camera slipping from her hand and her falling. She could not bring herself to admit what had started the whole episode. She was somehow ashamed that she had accidently seen the encounter between Spence and Darla. And if she weren't in such a safe yet ridiculous posture over his shoulder, she might have mustered a degree of anger and curiosity. Instead she felt cared for and protected. As they neared the farm out buildings, Spence transferred Cary to his arms. They were met by an anxious Mary and sleepy Agnes and Alice who would not retire until they saw for themselves that Cary was okay. Alice quickly brought a moist warm washcloth and tenderly wiped Cary's face and hands.

"I've got the 'wagon ready, Spence," Mary said, giving Cary a quick visual examination to assure herself that what the men and Cary said was true—no broken bones, no bad cuts. "And I can drive her in to the emergency room. You and Johnny are exhausted. Stay here and get some rest. It's practically breakfast time."

"You can drive, Mary," Spence acquiesced wearily, "but I'm going with you. No arguments. Let's get this blanket around Cary and go."

Cary added her feeble protests, but in very short order they had placed her in the back seat of Mary's battered station wagon, her leg outstretched and her head on a pillow in Spence's lap. He held her hand, being careful of the broken nails and the scratches. He had removed her watch, broken, and wrapped his handkerchief around the slightly cut wrist.

"Go ahead and close your eyes," he said. "It's a good twenty minutes to the hospital, even with Mary speeding!"

Mary gave Spence a fierce look but made no promises

about slowing down. "I'll try to miss any potholes. And traffic will be light this time of night."

By mid morning, Cary had been delivered back to Rosemary where Mary helped her into a demure flannel gown and tucked her into bed. She was adorned with a few bandages and several colorful bruises. According to the doctor, she was fortunate that her foot was just twisted and bruised, no bones broken. She had instructions to keep off the foot, to rest, and to take pain pills as needed. She drank the Farm's cold fresh water with gusto, ate a few bits of toast and fresh cheese, followed by hot cocoa. "We'll call your family later today," Mary told her. Then after much motherly fussing by the Grayson sisters, Cary fell into a sound and long sleep.

Dishes clattered loudly in the kitchen. Cary rubbed her eyes and came almost reluctantly back to reality. She'd been dreaming of a bright green restaurant where she dealt out solid heavy plates like cards in a poker game. The sounds of plates being shuffled and silverware being pulled from drawers were very real. She yawned widely and started to stretch, forgetting her soreness. "Ouch," she said loudly. "I must look awful." She looked around the room for a mirror.

"Could you bring me a mirror, please, Mary?" she called. "I must look like a witch."

No answer from the kitchen. Perhaps she had not been heard over all that noise of preparation or clean up. "Mary, could you get me the mirror from the bathroom? I feel like I've slept in a brush pile. My hair's a mess."

"This is no time, Cinderella, to be asking who's the fairest of them all!" Spence carried her mirror and a tray into the room. In clean jeans and a fatigue sweater, he appeared wide awake and alert. The sunlight struck his handsome features.

"Yipes," Cary put her hand to her mouth in surprise. "What are you doing here? Why aren't you sleeping?"

"I slept most of the day and it's now tea time." Spence put the tray on the bedside table and handed Cary the mirror.

"Yipes," she repeated. Her face was decidedly pale without makeup or lipstick, and her pumpknot was quite pronounced and blue-black.

"You don't look half bad," Spence assured her in a teasing drawl, "considering your bout with a blacksnake, a friendly cow, and a rock pile."

"Thanks, thanks a lot," Cary responded ruefully. Then more seriously, "I really do thank you—and Johnny—for finding me and lugging me out of there."

"All in the line of duty, ma'am. Just what any landlord would do." He poured a mug of steaming tea for himself. "You're a very lucky girl—person, you know. Lucky you didn't really crack your head or break a leg."

Cary nodded. Her eyes thanked him more than she might have wished. She reached for a brush and again realized just how battered her body was. A grimace crossed her face and she fell back on the plump pillow.

"Here, let me do that. I can see that you won't have your tea—ThymeTable's special brew—until you once again look ravishing." Spence took the brush and sat on the side of the bed. As naturally as if he performed this chore every day, he began to brush her short hair. He had not come off the mountain totally unscathed. His hands and arms bore many red roughened spots and some deep scratches. Cary relaxed as he brushed her hair and closed her eyes.

"Wake up, sleepyhead. Or you're going to suffer something like jet lag. You need to eat a little." Spence put the brush aside. "Here, we have special dark bread, straight from Mrs. Alison's oven, just for the invalid. Yep, everybody up and down the road knows of your escapade by now," he laughed. "And some more goat cheese and homemade apple butter from the annual stiroff of the Mt. Morenci Methodist Church two coves over."

He busied himself pouring tea. "You didn't have a lot in your refrigerator to work with. But Johnny's girlfriend Suzanne sent her special cookies. She baked up a batch especially to help Johnny recover from his night on the mountain. That Johnny better watch out!"

Cary bit hungrily into the chunk of bread that Spence had slathered with apple butter. The tea was perfect. Spence settled into the bedside chair which was almost too small for his frame and balanced his cup precariously on his knee while sampling a cookie.

Cary felt a curious embarrassment. She was thinking of their confrontation before her photography excursion, thinking that she had determined to leave ThymeTable and remembering why: Spence's distrust of her motives and his very reasonable dislike of Phillip's plans for the cove. None of that had changed. Yet here she was, still in his cottage, being "waited on hand and foot" as their cook Jemmie used to say. And Spence, cheerful, grinning, acting as if they were the best of buddies. She admitted to herself that she was enjoying his bedroom interlude, the first time he'd been in her bedroom, at least when she, Cary, was in it. Darla had undoubtedly slept here, but Cary refused at the moment to think about her. She felt pampered and supremely cared for. And that embarrassed her. She sipped the tea and sighed with appreciation.

"This is the same tea we had the first day I arrived," she remembered.

"As I said, my very special mix. I keep it for girls—"

"I am woman," Cary interrupted wickedly.

"Women," Spence grinned, "who find themselves in need of attention. They just keep falling—at least the same one just keeps needing my attention."

Cary knew he was joking, but the word "needing" provoked her instantly. Her face darkened.

Before she could say anything, partly because she had a mouthful of hot tea, Spence held up a hand before him as if to protect himself from the daggers in Cary's eyes. "Strike that!

Unfortunate choice of words. Don't get up! Remember, the doctor said to stay off your feet. I'm surely safe over here."

Cary said, after a moment, "Spence, all kidding aside, we have to talk." She sipped her tea and did not look at him. "I wanted to get pictures of those little Indian pipes and to get all the way up to See-Off, on my last day here at Rosemary. Now I'll have to stay a little longer . . . not much, actually. My parents can come—"

"Don't be a darn fool, Cary!" Spence exploded. "I told you to try staying and sticking it out, didn't I? Running away isn't going to solve anything."

"You're a fine one to talk, Spence Bradford. It's you— you—" Cary stopped, flushed. She couldn't let him know she was fleeing from him, her feelings for him, her realization that he was still very much attached to Darla. She turned her head aside. "I want to rest now."

"You, my dear tenant, started this. I was perfectly happy to lug you off the mountain and perfectly happy to feed you." Spence's voice had lost its tinge of anger and Cary thought he was almost teasing her. "You wanted to talk and now you want to rest. Okay, rest all you want. I'll be back in a couple of hours to check on you. Mary's in town with a client who couldn't be put off. She's got a big project in the works. I am taking care of you."

He stood up decisively. "And that is that."

"I've got to call my family," Cary said, retreating from his teasing and his concern.

"Did you tell them you'd be home today?" Spence placed the telephone on her bed, within easy reach.

"No. But I can't not let my mother and dad know I'm laid up here, even if I'm in the best of hands! And Phillip. Oh, Lord, Phillip will say the usual—"

"I told you so!" Both Cary and Spence chorused. Their laughter cleared the air of the tension.

Spence returned to the bed and picked up Cary's hand.

He studied the bandages and scratches. Cary almost held her breath. His touch was as gentle as if he were holding new plants, too young to be transplanted. His eyes still on her hand, and his voice husky, he said, "Cary, don't make any rash decisions right now. Stay here for a few more days at least. You aren't in the best frame of mind—or body to be finalizing anything. You'll be comfortable here. Promise me you'll not dash off in the middle of the night!"

"As if I could dash!" Cary kept her tone light, but she desperately wanted to promise to stay right there in Rosemary forever, close to Spence. But she saw again in her mind's eye Spence embracing not her but his beloved Darla, curvaceous Darla in the red dress, sexy blond hair flowing, arms around Spence.

Probably Darla was over at Spence's now, waiting for him while he was here, doing his landlordly bit. Even as the thought flashed across her mind, not for the first time, Cary both assumed it and yet doubted it. But Darla had been at ThymeTable yesterday . . . . or had she? Possibly the beautiful woman was someone else. Darla's name had not been mentioned on the trip to the hospital. Cary had to know.

"Spence, did you have a visitor yesterday while I was up on See-Off?"

Spence released her hand and looked levelly at Cary. Like a banker surveying his client, his eyes told her nothing. The silence was awkward. Inwardly Cary cringed that she had blurted out the question. Who came to the farm was certainly not her business, whether the visitor was female or lovely or a demon in disguise. She blushed and lowered her gaze.

"I'm sorry I asked," she said in a small, miserable voice. But inwardly she told herself she still wanted to know.

"Why did you ask, Cary? How could you even wonder? Did you also lose some binoculars on the mountain?" Even with his ironic question she could not determine whether he was angry or disgusted or simply irritated at her nosiness.

"Darla came back and you fell right into her arms, didn't you?" Cary was amazed at her brazenness, but she could not stay on at Rosemary, and face the reality of Darla at his house, in his arms, in his bed. In some strange way, she felt betrayed. She wanted Spence. She knew now that she loved him. Now when Darla was back. Like a coward, she turned her head aside and closed her eyes. She would not risk letting her eyes reveal her love, her foolishness. She would not lounge around ThymeTable like an invalid, waiting for Spence to introduce her to his Darla.

"Go. Go. She's probably impatient, wondering how long it takes you to feed your tenant. Just go." With her eyes closed Cary could not know that Spence was regarding her strangely, almost wonderingly.

"Oh, would some power the giftie gie us," she quoted in a firm voice, partly to fill the silence, "to see ourselves as others see us." This time she was thinking of herself and how incredibly silly she had been. "It would from many a blunder free us and foolish notion."

"A favorite quotation of yours, Cary the quoter. Just who is being the foolish one here? You want to talk, you don't want to talk, you ask questions, you don't want answers, and you think a neat quotation sums it up? And, damn, now you clamp your eyes shut." Spence strode to the door. He turned and spoke again, just as Cary's eyes flew open.

"This childish mood," he paused and repeated, "this mood—is surely the result of your painkillers or you could see a little more clearly. I'll ask Agnes to come over later to see if you need anything. And yes, Darla was here."

He was gone. And Cary wanted to pick up the telephone and throw it at his retreating back, his strong back, the back that had carried her with tenderness. Furious with herself and her questions—and his answer, she glared at the door. After a few moments, she resolutely dialed her home number to tell her family that once again she was incapacitated because of a fall.

"Darling, are you sure I can't help?" Cary's mother asked, after hearing about the accident. Cary had made light of the episode, as light as she could and still admit she was in bed. Then she surprised herself by declaring that she wanted to stay in bed a few more days even though she assured her mother she was fine. "We can come pick you up tomorrow. Dad and I—and we'd like to see the place."

"No, really, Mother. Last time we talked you said Dad was very busy this time of year." Cary loved her mother and her dad, but this time she had to work things out without their assistance. "A couple of days' rest and I'll be up taking pictures again." She described at length what she had been doing, and her enthusiasm must have convinced Mrs. Randall that Cary wasn't in dire need of their comfort.

"But, I do want you both to come out to this end of the state this summer. It's beautiful, especially now that all the flowers are out." Cary realized that she truly did feel at home in western North Carolina. But would she want to remain in or around Asheville if she weren't at ThymeTable? She didn't want to answer that question.

"And is someone there to look after you?"

"Mother," Cary protested, "yes. Mary is wonderful and so is . . . everyone. Besides, I just sprained the ankle. Now I just have to take it easy for a few days."

Cary's mother made her promise they would talk every day until Cary was fully back on her feet. "Now I have a question for you, Mother," Cary said.

"Anything, darling," replied Ruthlene. "Are you going to ask if I'm making Dad take his medicine? The answer is yes and he's golfing every weekend."

"No. It's about Phillip. Is he there?"

"What do you mean? No, he isn't here—in the house— at the moment. Do you want me to have him call you?"

"No. I mean, is he in town? Or away on business? What is he doing these days? How is Suntip Beach doing?"

"I don't know about Suntip," her mother answered, puzzled. "And I believe he has another big project lined up. Or he's working on it." She thought for a moment. "In fact, he and Alecia have been gone recently, but they come and go so often that I don't always know where they are. I've had my bridge club and the auxiliary this week, so . . . They were here for dinner . . . oh, last weekend. Why?"

Cary recognized her mother's usual vagueness about Phillip's business deals. She was not being coy; she simply did not pay much attention to her husband's and her son's activities outside the home.

"Just curious, that's all. Denise is still trying to sell her Suntip condo, and I wondered." After more reassurances and promises to eat right, rest, and call every day, Cary replaced the phone. More tired than she had let on to her mother, Cary drifted into a semi-sleep until Agnes dropped by to check on her.

"I'm putting this soup on to heat," Agnes announced as she came in the back door. "From what Spence said, he plied you with carbs and sweets mostly. You need something nourishing. Black bean soup it is. I'll give you the recipe."

"Thanks, Agnes. Will you eat with me?" Cary propped herself up. "I had some of your delicious goat cheese in addition to the cookies and apple butter. But that soup smells wonderful."

"Here you are." The older woman bustled in. "Alice and I have long since eaten. I'm glad you've got your color back." She cocked her head to one side. "Quite a bit of color in some places."

Cary laughed and began to eat her soup. "I'm sorry I caused all of you so much trouble."

"No trouble at all, child. We were worried to death about

you, that's the truth. But Alice said we could trust Spence and Johnny to find you. Once we knew you were gone and not out gallivanting with some beau in town!"

"Oh, Agnes, I don't have a beau in town."

"Well, you were mighty dressed up the other night," Agnes reminded her, "when you went into town."

"No beau," Cary said again.

"Well, it's not for lack of interest, is it?" Agnes smoothed the bed linen. "Have you seen Justin lately? He is certainly a good-looking boy."

"No Justin," Cary replied. Her eyes twinkled. "Keep trying."

"Justin is awfully busy doctoring. And he's bound and determined to make scads of money before he's dry behind the ears!" Agnes eyed the resting girl.

Cary laughed again. She knew that Agnes and Alice loved to tease her, and both sisters had picked up many local expressions with which they sometimes liberally peppered their conversation. In her expressive manner of speaking, if not in her accent, Agnes could have passed for a native western North Carolinian.

"Justin is surely a very good doctor," Cary kept her voice neutral. "And he probably will make scads of money."

"Doctors need a good wife to help them spend all that money," Agnes continued as innocently as a robin about to snatch a bean bug.

"My friend Denise can certainly spend money," Cary rejoined.

"Denise—fenise!" declared Agnes. "Have you called Justin about your accident?"

Cary had not even thought about Justin, and she did not intend to call him at this hour. In fact, she had not intended to call him at all. Perhaps she should. He would be hurt to find out later that she had not thought of him at least as a friend. As only a friend, Cary reminded herself.

"No, I haven't called him," she told Agnes. "Maybe tomorrow when I'm more alert. This hot soup is halfway putting me to sleep, and I've already slept most of the day."

Agnes took the hint. "I'll fix you a cup of our very special tea. It will help you relax and sleep."

Cary started to protest, but Agnes had already gone into the kitchen to boil water. A strange odor wafted into the bedroom, followed soon by Agnes with a mug in her hand.

"It may not be especially appealing to your nose, Cary, but this will help. It's an old remedy for calming nerves."

"What is it?" The odor was not especially enticing. "My nerves are okay," she added.

"It's made from the dried root of Valerian. Don't sniff. Just drink." She straightened Cary's bed and nodded encouragement as she sipped the brew. "Occasionally sister and I have a cup if our old bones are threatening to keep us awake too long. We make it cold, but I thought you'd like this better."

"Ugh," responded Cary. "I can't say that I love the taste. Valerian, huh? I've never heard of it."

Agnes went to the other room and brought back Cary's large herbal encyclopedia, a recent purchase of which she was very fond. In preparing the tea, however, Agnes had not forgotten their conversation.

"Remember to call Justin tomorrow." After tidying up, she left Cary with only a few more motherly instructions.

Cary read in her herbal encyclopedia about Valerian, its early uses as a sedative and as perfume, how to concoct the "cold tea" version, and how to recognize it. But before she finished she realized the tea was indeed doing its work. She laid the book aside and turned out her light.

Chapter 10

The next morning, Mary helped Cary with her morning showering, assisting her as she awkwardly hopped about. Cary wanted to sit in the kitchen, but Mary insisted that she return to bed and allow her to bring more coffee and breakfast.

"Please, just cold cereal, Mary. I won't be burning very many calories for a few days, and almost all I remember after the hospital yesterday is being fed." Cary recalled quite clearly Spence's defensiveness. She wondered what their next encounter would bring? Darla was probably having breakfast right now with Spence. Preparing him an herb-flavored omelet or watching him prepare it? Was he entertaining her with the story of his tenant's foolish fall and his heroic rescue? To be honest Cary did not think Spence would make fun of her or her accident. But she squirmed restlessly before being diverted by the large bowl of cornflakes and fresh strawberries that Mary set before her.

"Spence has gone to the Farmers' Market to see about the herb festival. He's got a booth lined up, but there are some details to check out. He said he'd be out most of the day." Mary stretched her long legs and sipped her coffee.

"By himself?" Cary spoke through a mouthful of flakes. Another vision of Spence and Darla wandering hand in hand through the large bustling market, intimately choosing vegetables and browsing through the craft items sent a frown across her face.

"In pain?" Mary asked with concern. "Let me get you something for it."

"No, no, I'm not hurting," replied Cary. Not physically anyway. Well, not much. The image of Spence and Darla together did bring a very real heaviness to her chest, but she wasn't going to reveal that pain to Mary.

With a speculative gaze, Mary answered Cary's question. "Yes, alone. Johnny's at the garage."

The silence was broken only by the sounds of cornflakes being devoured. Mary seemed to be waiting. Finally she said, somewhat sharply, "Obviously you know Darla was at the farm while you were at See-Off. She left sometime in the late afternoon. And I don't know what time she had arrived. Now, what else do you want to know?"

Cary cringed at the rebuke in her friend's voice. Clearly Mary had a low opinion of Darla, but she apparently didn't exactly approve of Cary's interest in Spence either. In her eyes, Cary thought, I must come across as a silly fool here for the summer, another woman pursuing her good friend, just another woman who would hurt him.

Cary's voice was shaky; tears welled up. "Oh, Mary, don't be angry with me. I know what Spence does and who he does it with is none of my business. I know that, and I wouldn't hurt him . . ." She stopped. Why should she presume that she could hurt him? Pretty presumptuous on her part.

"You wouldn't hurt him, Cary?" Mary turned back to the girl. "Wouldn't you?"

"No, I couldn't, I mean how could I? He told me," Cary's lip trembled. She looked as forlorn as a six-year-old who has just been sent her to her room in disgrace. "He told me I wasn't in Darla's league. I'm just . . . I'm just . . . , just here. Oh, darn," she said. "Please hand me a Kleenex. I'm more upset by yesterday's adventure than I thought."

Mary handed her a soft, scented tissue. "That or something," she said.

Cary blew her nose with an exaggerated fury, and blinked away a tear. She wanted suddenly to be in her own canopy bed—not in her apartment—back at her parents' home. Her mother would comfort her. Phillip would deal with her problems, and her Dad would sympathize no matter what she had done or not done. It would be so easy to return to her pampered existence, an existence when everything—except Lanny—had been smoothed by her family and their love. Then she had allowed herself to be treated like a child, had possibly encouraged it. She remembered a line from the poet Shelley: "I could lie down like a tired child and weep." Well, Cary thought with determination, I am no child and I'll not weep. I can handle my emotional state—if not my physical one—without help.

Mary removed the breakfast tray. "Not in Darla's league, huh?"

"She's beautiful and sexy and clever and . . ." Cary ran out of adjectives. She still knew very little about Darla. She knew more about the nurse in Senegal.

"Yes," Mary said, "She's all that—and more." With that cryptic comment she went into the kitchen, leaving Cary to squirm once again into a more comfortable position.

I'm not at home, Cary reminded herself. Nobody is going to "fix" this situation for me. And I wasn't pushed into that rock pile. This time I have only myself to blame and only myself to repair the damage. Her bruises would heal soon, but the damage to her heart was another matter.

Mary called over the sound of dishes clattering, "And you don't think you could hurt Spence?"

"No, I don't!" retorted Cary. "What makes you think otherwise?"

"Oh, nothing," came the unsatisfactory reply. Then, "I am getting some things together for your lunch. One of the sisters will be over. I have to go back to my client."

Mary poked her head around the corner, a teasing glint in her eyes. "I declare, Cary, most of this spring I've been underbooked, and now that you get yourself incapacitated and need a nurse of sorts, my luck turns and this manuscript has to be finished in double quick time. You have brought me luck!"

"Sure. Thanks. I'll be happy to fall into a hole anytime. Just call."

"If this project works out," Mary continued more seriously, "and it looks good, the company wants a series of reports. Enough to make me think I've got a steady job instead of freelancing."

"That's great, Mary. I want to hear all about it."

The telephone rang. Mary handed the receiver to her.

"Hello. Oh, hi, Justin."

Mary noted the friendly lilt in Cary's voice as she waved goodby.

"I'm fine, really. Being pampered and fed constantly. By Mary and the Grayson sisters. No, nothing's broken," Cary assured him. "Well, my pride is severely damaged, and my body is pretty sore."

Cary gave Justin an abbreviated version of her adventure on the mountain and a full version of the medical treatment to satisfy his doctoring questions.

"Enough about me," she finished. "How are you? How is Denise? Are you properly appreciative of her talents?" Now, wondered Cary cynically, exactly what do I mean by that?

"I'm working hard. Denise is busy on a show for early September on the coast. And she does have an extraordinary eye for beauty and for bringing it out in her jewelry," Justin responded smoothly. Hmmmm, Cary thought. Maybe Denise has finally found a man who sympathizes with her bursts of hard work and her dedication to her business.

"It's you I want to talk to and to see," Justin went on. "I can wrangle a weekend free to come check on you."

"That's very sweet of you, Justin," Cary said, "but really I am okay except for selected bruises and a sprained ankle." Realizing she might sound ungracious, she continued, "It would be nice to see you."

"I need to check on Dad's place too. And decide what to do about it."

"Do? You aren't thinking of getting out of the cove, are you?" Cary still didn't understand exactly how her neighbors were bound together legally, but surely if Justin wanted out, their position in resisting an offer from any developer or from Phillip would be weakened.

"It's always been a possibility," Justin said vaguely. "I'd probably never return there to live, and maintaining the house as vacation home . . . well, you know I prefer the beach." Justin paused. "Would you be glad to see me, Cary?"

"Another doctor to tend to me?" Cary laughed. She did not want to read more into the simple question than Justin might have meant. "Of course, I'll be glad to see you. And I want to hear all about you and Denise!"

The silence on the other end of the phone lasted only a few seconds. Then Justin said, "I'll see you in a couple of days. Don't go anywhere!"

"Bye, Justin. Thanks for calling. I'll be right here." Did Justin feel guilty about his relationship with Denise? Did he expect Cary to be more than routinely glad to see him? Was he trying to decide which to pursue: Cary or Denise? While Cary was mulling over the call, the telephone rang again.

Cary spent most of the morning talking. Mark offered to pick up her film and develop it for her since it would be some time before she could stand for hours developing and printing her pictures. He and his wife appeared around eleven and were still visiting and talking photography when Alice came in to prepare a late lunch for the invalid. They got up to take their leave, promising to call and report on the photographs.

"You're getting better and better at 'seeing' what you see," Mark complimented her. "Nature photography seems to come naturally to you."

More naturally now that I've practiced so many hours and days," Cary agreed. "I still love the textures of wood and stone, the old barns, fences, mills."

"With some advanced darkroom work, by next spring you could have a show ready for one of the downtown galleries," Mark said. His wife nodded enthusiastically.

"Oh no. I've not thought that far ahead. But I have high hopes for at least one contest I've entered." Cary flushed with pleasure at Mark's assessment. She wasn't at all sure she was ready to go public with her hobby. Not for awhile at least. And the chances of her being in Asheville the following spring weren't very promising. She closed her eyes for a moment.

"We're tiring her," Mark's wife, Lisa, observed. "Let's get out of here so she can rest."

They said their farewells, taking a sample of goat cheese which Alice pressed on them.

Alice wanted to hear about the results of the Valerian tea, and Cary reported that it certainly seemed to have worked. She'd slept soundly and awakened refreshed.

After the light lunch of chicken salad, Cary said, "Tell me more about local wild herbs and your home brewed concoctions."

Cary propped herself up for a comfortable session. "I've heard about ginseng, but just from books. Have you ever found any? Does it grow on this mountain?"

"Ginseng grows all over these mountains. We've never been very successful at finding it above our place, but it's probably there. Mrs. Alison can remember when people used to find it. She thinks they took too much and it's pretty much gone now. Still sister and I keep looking every time we go up there." Alice sighed. "We're getting a little old to do much serious herbing. We have to plant what we want where we can see it! Do you know what 'sang looks like?"

"I've seen pictures." Cary opened her encyclopedia to the page with its drawing. "I'd really like to find some for myself."

"This fall's the time to go looking. That's when you can more easily spot the red berries that are left after the flowers go."

"Listen to what one early gatherer said about it," Cary read. "I carried home this Treasure, with as much Joy as if every Root had been the Graft of the Tree of Life."

"Yes," Alice settled down. "Of course, they thought it would cure just about everything from headaches to female disorders to male disorders! Especially the last. It was touted then—and still is—especially as an aphrodisiac."

"According to this," Cary continued, "over half a million pounds of the dried roots were exported in one year in 1876! Somebody believed in it."

"And people still believe in it," Alice said. "I admit I've never had any man specifically admit to its powers, but herbal cures or impotency, for that matter, weren't topics of conversation in our teachers' lounge."

"It says here that you can buy seeds and maybe get a crop started."

"A long process and a tricky one, with more failures than successes," Alice said. "It's a very particular plant, not one to be tamed or civilized in a garden. A friend of ours on the other side of the county does some harvesting on her family's mountainside. She knows how to take it and how to leave enough behind. They have their land specifically posted against 'sang hunters, and still they have to get their shot-guns out every fall and patrol the boundaries."

At Cary's raised eyebrows, Alice admitted, "Well, they don't really patrol, but occasionally they'll scare a poacher or two."

"I've always wanted to find a complete sand dollar at the beach," Cary mused, "And I never have. Now I would like to find a patch of ginseng. Just to see it growing."

"We'll ask the Burdettes if you can go with them this fall when they go 'sanging," Alice said. "I'm sure they wouldn't mind, provided your intentions are pure."

"Purely looking, that's all I'd want," Cary promised.

"The root is sometimes shaped like a man, as you can see." Alice pointed to the picture. "That is surely one reason the ancients expected so much of it. Who knows whether it is really as potent in so many ways as is claimed? Or whether the expectation leads to results."

"Ah, the skeptic," said Cary.

"The undecided," Alice said. "We've bought ginseng tea at various times in our travels, but other than a general pick-me-up I couldn't vouch for anything else. In fact, there will undoubtedly be some ginseng tea for sale at the herb festival in Asheville."

Alice lingered until late afternoon, telling Cary about the festival and about other, less highly regarded herbs that she and her sister valued. Cary almost forgot that she had not seen or heard from Spence the entire day.

"Justin called this morning," she reported. "And he's coming down this weekend."

"Worried about you, is he?"

"A little, I guess. He's also got to check on his Dad's house and maybe decide what to do with it."

"That young man is getting ready to settle down. All those years in medical school, I'm surprised he wasn't nabbed by some pretty young thing. Now he's in a practice, he'll be looking to get married, mark my words."

"Maybe," Cary conceded. "He and my friend Denise are seeing each other—when they're not too busy."

"Does your friend have money of her own?"

"Family money, you mean? No. Her dad's dead. He was a supervisor in the big factory in her hometown. Her mother works as an office manager in a large dental office. Why?"

"Just old-woman curious." Alice busied herself rearranging pillows and other items around the room.

"No, tell me why you asked," Cary insisted. "Denise has a very good jewelry design business. I wouldn't be surprised if she hits pay dirt in a few years. Some of her pieces have been featured in the glossy women's magazines and one movie star paid quite a sum for a specially-designed piece when she was on location in Virginia and saw Denise's work."

Alice listened attentively but seemed inclined to say nothing more.

"Are you trying to tell me something about Justin?"

"I was just curious, that's all. But Justin does like the good life. He won't be driving that old Volvo much longer."

"And?"

"And I can't see him getting too interested in a poor girl." Alice pursed her lips sagely. "That's why he didn't fall for a nurse all during his training. He wants more than a working girl."

"Alice, I'm ashamed of you! Lots of medical students don't get married during their training. You aren't being your usual analytical self." She wagged her finger at the elderly woman who had the grace to look chagrined but not daunted. Cary went on, "That same logic would explain Spence's bachelor status. And what about me? Surely you don't assume that I'm not married because I haven't found someone with a lot of money! Really, Alice."

Alice tossed her gray head with its short, crisp curls. "Well, young lady, what have you been waiting for? Some poor man who needs you?"

Before Cary could formulate a retort, a strong male chuckle made both women turn to the door. Spence stood there, a large bouquet of daffodils in his hand, his eyes taking in Cary in her long pink tee shirt. Her left foot was swollen and bare, and the other foot sported a fluffy, white, bunny house shoe. Cary's mother had bought those bunny slippers and had explained, somewhat surprisingly, "I've read an article on comfort food. These are comfort bedroom shoes. You might need them." Mary, rummaging in the closet this morning, had found the bunnies.

"Lord, Miss Alice," he asserted, "you have said the wrong thing now. Waiting for someone who needs her? Cary? She refuses to recognize the word! Pity the poor man who ever needs Cary."

He handed the flowers to Alice. "A peace offering. There's a vase in the kitchen in the right-hand cupboard."

"Spence, don't mock me," Cary flared. Her face was hot.

"Or is it the other way around?" he went on, more serious now. "You don't intend to need anybody to make you happy. You are beyond need—at least today."

A wave of absolute desire had swept over Cary when she saw him, in well-worn jeans and a bomber jacket, in the doorway. She wanted him to rush to the bed and take her in his arms. Instead he was the considerate visitor, bringing flowers no less, probably from the market, probably chosen by Darla. He was also keeping a safe distance, leaning against the doorframe, his hands now in his pockets. His taunting words stung her. But she could hardly deny that she had needed him—or someone—to rescue her. And here she lay in his cottage at his mercy. Loving him, wanting him, and losing him to Darla.

"Speechless? Not even a quotation?" Spence looked toward a chair. "May I come in?"

"Of course! It's your house, isn't it? Please," she emphasized the pleasantry, "make yourself at home."

Alice returned with the golden flowers in a stylized triangular piece of pottery. As she placed them on the dresser, she told Cary, "Jon's pottery. Unexpected shape. Like Jon—always the unexpected."

Spence looked with appreciation at the flowers. Then his eyes returned to Cary and, flushed, she snapped her attention from him to the daffodils.

Alice said pertly, "Justin called. He's coming down this weekend."

"Damn Justin," Spence swore quietly. "Sorry, Alice. That slipped out." He ran his hand through his hair. "Coming to do some doctoring of his own for you, Cary?"

"I assured him that I am okay," she said. "He needs to check on his dad's place."

"Sure, he makes it a practice to check in here on his every free day, does he?" Spence drawled.

"Don't you like him, Spence?" Cary had assumed that no seeds of discord had ever sprouted among the neighbors.

"I like Justin," Spence said. "Since I bought this place, he hasn't been here much so I never got to know him very well, not like his father." Cary wondered at the reserve in Spence's tone. "He knows what he wants," he continued, "and I have to admire that in anybody."

"But?"

"But what he wants is another matter." Spence took a cup of coffee that Alice brought to him. He sipped carefully, his teasing glance telling Alice that he recognized her tendency to make strong coffee and serve it blisteringly hot.

"Tell me about the market today. Is everything set for the festival? It's the weekend after this one, isn't it?"

"Things are pretty much under control," he answered. "Just some routine details to work out."

"Spence! I could have some photographs enlarged.

Mark could blow up some to four or five feet for a backdrop for your booth. That would attract attention!"

"That's a great idea, Cary." He gave her a quick, decisive nod. He also seemed to relax at the change of subject. "We'll have some giveaways. They're always a crowd-pleaser. I have ThymeTable pencils ordered. And then I thought just the usual ThymeTable Farm banner, but pictures—big ones—would be different. I could build some screens."

"Or maybe hang them free form—on big pieces of Styrofoam." Cary's eyes flashed with enthusiasm.

"Our—" With a quick look at the reclining girl, Spence corrected himself, "My booth—the farm's booth is at the upper end of the market, and there are exposed beams, open rafters of steel. They're fairly high, but if we weighted the pictures to keep them from being too free floating—yes, that would work."

"I'll get some of my herb pictures," Cary unthinkingly started from the bed. Her movements told her just how sore and aching her body was. Wincing, she again settled back against the pillow.

"Where are they? I'll get them," said Alice. "Then I've got to go help with the goats. Sister will have a hard time forgiving me for staying so long. She's brewing up a special concoction."

"In the living room, the box near the door, I think." Cary said with mock despair, "I have pictures all over this cottage. What I must do is start filing and labeling, especially before my mother gets here!"

"Stay put, Cary. Filing and labeling can wait." Spence hitched his chair close to the bed. "That was a hard fall you took. Give yourself some time—and lots of hot baths."

"Yes sir," Cary grunted. She wished she had put on something more feminine than this fuchsia tee shirt and the bunny shoe. She was also very much aware that the shirt surely revealed her braless state, yet she could hardly pull a sheet up around her on this warm evening. Well, Spence had certainly seen nipples and tee shirts before. She shifted to a more comfortable position, pulling the shirt even tighter over her thighs. My best bet, she thought, is to stay put. Spence was very close to the bed. He seemed perfectly oblivious to her plight as he took the box of photographs from Alice.

With reluctance Alice said goodbye. "I left the bean soup on the stove and makings for sandwiches in the refrigerator, and I'll be sure to check on you tomorrow." Cary smiled and waved. Then she returned her attention to the pile of photographs between them on the edge of the bed.

"These are good, Cary," murmured Spence. "Some are very good. This one of thyme especially. How did you get so close and capture that little blue flower. That's not thyme, but it makes the picture better. I can almost smell it."

"Smell! That's something else. We could—could we—somehow get the scent of the herbs sprayed close to the pictures?"

"Have you ever thought about being in advertising?" Spence asked. "Yes, I could surely manage some sort of odor-wafting machine! Maybe a fan."

"And a pot or pots of simmering herbs! We could change the pots during the day and bring people back again and again." Cary visualized huge photos swinging in a breeze, natural or fan-made, with wonderful aromas surrounding the booth. "Of course, people could be drawn to our—your booth and still buy next door."

"The luck of the draw," Spence admitted. "If they buy from competitors, at least they buy. Next time might be my time. Your ideas are great, Cary. Let's pick out some other shots. What do you think. Four or five?"

"Probably five would be about right. Too many would be overkill—and we don't want them to get tangled up when they're hanging from the beams. We could use some others in eight by ten format on screens—with some commentary, either educational or anecdotal. Suzanne is an accomplished calligrapher, did you know that? I bet she'd be happy to do the lettering. And Alice has all kind of tales about various herbs." Cary laughed. "You should get her started on ginseng!"

"Ah, the mighty ginseng—fabled in legend and imagination. I tried to grow some from seed, but no luck. It takes an infernal long time to germinate—sometimes eighteen or more months. And then years to get marketable roots. Besides, my experiment just didn't work. I added bone meal and did all I could but the plants died a quick death." Spence placed several photographs in a row on the bed and studied them intently. His hand was very close to Cary's bunny-shod foot.

"And what got you started on ginseng? Someone you know been asking about it? Someone think you're a potential source since you're at an herb farm?" His drawl had taken on a deliberately sensual huskiness, and his fingers edged closer to the bunny's flop ears. "Phillip checking on it?"

Cary smiled sweetly although her heart was on alert and her pulse racing. "Not to worry. No one has asked me about the perky plant. I would like to see it growing in the wild— just to see it. Alice told me about the Burdettes' place. Maybe I can go 'sang hunting this fall."

Even as she said it, Cary's face fell. She uttered a little "Oh." She wouldn't be at ThymeTable this fall. She had totally forgotten her resolve to leave in her excitement over the herb festival. And Spence had let her run on, ignoring the fact that she had told him she would be leaving as soon as she recovered and could walk without hobbling. What a fool she'd been. She had insisted she was leaving, and then she had simply forgotten.

Spence said nothing now. He must have realized what her "Oh" meant. If by no other means, the shamefaced expression and flush on her cheeks. He was not looking at her.

His hand had reached the fluffy bunny and his fingers were twining around the ears. Then they touched her bare flesh. Soft, warm, tentative, the touch sent a shock through her. He stroked the top of her foot, slowly, his eyes on the discarded bunny shoe that he had adroitly slipped off. His other hand was on his knee, as if glued or he didn't yet dare activate it. He traced designs toward her toes and slipped his fingers to the sole. Cary usually could not bear to have her feet tickled. But this highly charged current that raced through her and then stayed with her was nothing like being tickled. Spence bent his head and rubbed his cheek, stubbly, along the foot; his eyes were hooded, and his breath was warm, warm on her instep. Turning his face slightly, he left light kisses on each toe, kisses so extraordinarily gossamer light that Cary wondered if she'd imagined them. She could be still no longer. A low moan escaped her.

The sound seemed all the invitation Spence needed. He moved his lips across her foot and toward her ankle, still as delicately as butterfly wings in a fantasy. The effect made Cary writhe with longing. She did not bend toward him. Such was her position that any motion on her part would disturb his progress. His lips touched, withdrew, touched with the rhythm of a stone skipping lightly on smooth waters.

I just might swoon, Cary thought, surprising herself with the word, a word she'd encountered often in stories of King Arthur when under powerful emotions, queens and princesses swooned easily. She and her classmates had rolled their eyes at such descriptions. Let Guenevere swoon at the sight of Lancelot. They were too sophisticated for that kind of behavior. A swoon was a graceful losing of oneself in pure bliss or pure sorrow or pure pain. At this moment she understood about pure bliss—but she didn't swoon.

Spence's lips had nudged the tee shirt higher and he paused, tantalizingly and deliberately. With great finesse he kissed the inside of her knee. In fact, she realized the kiss was prolonged and was turning noisy. He was teasing her! With a last flick of his tongue he pursed his lips to emit a resounding smack.

When he raised his eyes, he was smiling broadly, totally satisfied with himself. "Ah, Cary," he said, "You are the most desirable little temptress. Lying there with one foot twice its normal size and sexy as all hell in a god-awful shirt. What is a man supposed to do?"

"You did very well," Cary said, her breathing almost back to normal. She couldn't resist continuing, "Just what did you intend to do?"

"Nothing. Absolutely nothing. I intended to behave perfectly. Guess I lost my head."

"Since I'm so sexy, yeah," Cary said.

"I intended to be businesslike—"

"It was the talk about ginseng that did it." Cary adjusted her tee shirt. Maybe he hadn't heard her moan. Let him assume she wasn't bothered by his playacting.

"Ginseng is overrated as a stimulus," Spence returned. He pulled his chair close to her pillow and she knew he intended to kiss her properly. She closed her eyes in anticipation. His hand cupped her chin.

The telephone jangled—very close to their heads.

"Damn," both muttered simultaneously. Spence jerked back.

"Hello," she managed. "Yes, he's here. Just a moment." She handed the telephone to Spence who stood up.

"Hello. Who? Jon?"

Cary sat upright and swung her feet to the edge of the bed, keeping the sprained foot from the floor. She was surprised that the elusive Jon was calling but she didn't want to eavesdrop, so she intended to go into the bathroom. She also wished to regain some degree of composure. And she hoped her face did not mirror the disappointment in her heart that the promised kiss had not materialized.

The call itself lasted less than five minutes, and Cary heard only Spence's almost monosyllabic but positive responses to a more talkative Jon: "Good. Okay. Great. Sure. Sure. Yeah," and more yeses.

When he put the phone down, Spence announced his news. "Jon's come into some money. Just like him. It fell into his lap when some company wanted to purchase a so-called worthless piece of land that Jon picked up for a song—maybe for a gambling debt somebody owed him—over ten years ago. Now his land is just where a major industry needs a right-of-way."

Spence paused dramatically. "The long and short is," he said, "Jon is investigating the legalities of buying the land here in the Cove and—"

"What?" Cary interjected.

"And," Spence continued calmly, "setting up some sort of land trust so that everybody, everybody who wants to, can stay on here as long as they live."

"Oh," breathed Cary in relief, "then Alice and Agnes would be okay. They aren't ready to move to a retirement home. Not yet says Alice."

"Not ever says Agnes," finished Spence. "Jon, in spite of his wayward and roaming ways, is generous to a fault when he has anything. He just doesn't try very hard to have anything. Mary would be assured of a place as long as she wants it, as well as the sisters. Ultimately, he says, he'd want the land to be administered as some sort of preserve, some sort of domesticated wilderness. Right now he's got a law firm that specializes in saving wetlands and wilderness areas checking it all out. He'll finish up some business in Mexico before he can come to visit—maybe this fall. But once the details are clear, he'll be in touch again."

"Great!" Cary's grin matched Spence's. They both looked out the window at the land beyond.

"Let Phillip stew awhile on this deal, will you, Cary. I don't believe he could get the big guys in Asheville to absolutely commit themselves before Jon makes his offer. And, of course, Mary and the others, or most, would want to reject it anyway, but right now, let's keep Jon's situation quiet."

Spence looked at her. "It won't hurt your relationship with Phillip, will it?"

"Of course not!" Cary replied with some indignation. "I tried to tell you that Phillip and I are not tied up in this deal of his. I hate the thought of the Cove becoming a golf complex or whatever. Somebody's face is going to be red, though, after the article in the paper."

"No. Stories like that come and go. There's always somebody who's going to do great things for the region—to improve its economy and fix all its problems big time and at the same time not interfere with its pristine natural quality. The only red face may be Phillip's but he's used to property deals falling through. That's part of the game."

"And Mary?" asked Cary. "Will she take that kind of help from Jon? She doesn't seem to have any hostility toward him, but—"

"I think she'll be fine with it. Jon will wait until he's sure before he tells her the situation. The scheme will save the land the way she wants it. And it will certainly free her from a financial burden, so she can travel more or indulge in grandmotherly activities."

"What? Grandmotherly? Do you know something I don't? Have Johnny and—?"

"Not yet," admitted Spence with a knowing smile. "But any fool can see it's coming. And Johnny's likely to move to town to be closer to the garage and to school."

"He's so young. They are both young. I don't know about marriage." Cary said. "I bet they wait."

Spence cast his eyes heaven-ward. "Bet you—hmmmmm. I bet you two more months at ThymeTable, here in Rosemary, that Johnny's married before Christmas. And a father soon thereafter!"

"Two months more here," Cary stuttered in surprise. For a long moment, she pretended to be considering the bet and not all its implications. She propped her chin on her fist, contemplation-style. "Well, okay. I may very well lose, but you know I'm a betting woman. Still I must go visit my parents soon. Or they'll be here to check on me."

Spence nodded, then yawned. "It's been a long day. Let's shake on the bet. I don't want you reneging on me."

"In the spring a young man's fancy lightly turns to thoughts of love," quoted Cary. "But marriage?"

"Marriage. That's Johnny's way." Spence took her extended hand and gave it a gentlemanly shake. "We'll talk more about the photographs tomorrow. You need to get some rest, and I've got some thinking to do." With a mock bow he left the cottage.

Chapter 11

"Hi, Cary!" Justin leapt from his yellow Volvo. In his crisp, white shirt, sleeves rolled up at the cuffs and his dark cotton trousers, he would have been perfectly at home at any Club Med resort. His hair shone like a golden halo in the early morning sunshine.

Cary was lazing in sheer comfort with cushions under her foot, behind her back, supporting her head. Everyone insisted on either bringing her tea or settling another cushion around her. She felt quite capable now of doing for herself, but Agnes and Alice derived such pleasure from mothering her that she gave in with only token protest.

Justin hastened across the lawn to the shaded patio. Scattering cushions haphazardly, she rose to greet him. She aimed for his cheek; he aimed a kiss toward her lips. They laughed at the result.

"You're looking great. No visible damage." Justin held her hands and surveyed her with non-professional warmth.

"Still fairly colorful in places," Cary grinned. "Most of which you don't see! But, yes, I'm certainly mending. With this cane I can get around okay." She gestured at all the books, teapot and cups, magazines close by. "Not that anyone lets me do much! Mary and the sisters treat me like Ms. Queen Bee around here. You'd think they feel responsible for the snake on that rock!"

"Nobody else helping?" asked Justin. He brought a lawn chair closer to Cary.

"My brother Phillip and Alecia have been out. Lots of good advice from them. They're gone now." Phillip was provoked that nothing was happening with his property deal. Yet already he had begun negotiations with a South Carolina group to buy an ailing RV Park and turn it into a prestigious resort. Alecia did not allow much grass to grow under Phillip's well-shod feet.

"Gone?" Justin's question had an edge to it. Was he wondering about the possibility, or lack of it, of selling his property to Phillip and his developer buddies?

"For now, anyway."

"Tell me about your fall, Cary." For the next several minutes, they talked about Cary's photography excursion and accident. Justin examined her ankle and pronounced that all was as it should be. Cary could have been in any doctor's office for all the emotion his touch evoked.

Now, admiring Justin's perfectly coiffured head Cary wondered if he would sell his section of the Cove to Jon outright. As if he read her thoughts, Justin said, "I must make a decision soon about the property, Dad's place." He never referred to the land as his place.

"It doesn't mean a great deal to you?" Cary asked.

"No," returned Justin. "I simply am not attached to it, beyond the memory of my dad. This," he gazed at the farm and surrounding mountains, "this is not my spot. I like the city. Where there's more to do than count the clouds and shift the soil. Surely you're the same way, Cary. Admit it, haven't you gotten bored out here?"

"Barrymore's a fairly small town, Justin, so I have never

lived in a big city. I am truly content here." She looked directly at him. "I could shift the soil a long time without being bored. Or, at least, I could photograph it!"

"You're too sophisticated to mean that, Cary!" Justin sounded as if he could not quite believe she could live, actually live, rather than simply retreat, here. A change came over his countenance, almost like a shift in gears.

"Sophisticated?" Cary smiled. "I hardly think liking to be out here equals a lack of sophistication, Justin. Your dad was content here, learned, well-read, and well-traveled as he was!"

"You know what I mean, Cary," Justin refused to back down. "There's a limit to—I mean, how many concerts and plays can you see around here?"

Cary opened her mouth to tell him just how many, but he threw up his hands and said quickly, "No! Don't start! There's no winning on this issue. I just prefer a city at least as big as Charlotte or Norfolk."

Cary settled back and let a small silence descend. She looked at her fingernails, unpolished and short. They had not yet recovered from her fall.

"Where would Denise like to live?" she asked.

"Denise needs lots of contacts to keep her business going," Justin replied warily. "Not necessarily New York or somewhere like that, but she likes a city with lots of boutiques and fine shops. I know—Asheville's got that, and she says she wouldn't mind living here."

Justin sounded skeptical. "But I, not me. Thirty minutes to get a good cup of cappuccino! I had enough of this winding road as a teenager. No more gravel roads for me." He flashed Cary a smile, "Dad was a sort of Thoreau, maybe, but I need the fast lane!"

"And?" In Justin's visit Cary sensed an undercurrent of things unsaid. Was Justin attempting to determine her interest in him? Was he trying to tell her that he and Denise could—if she showed no interest—be a couple? Was he trying to diagnose without asking the necessary questions so he wouldn't hurt the "patient" if he guessed wrong? Was Justin angling for a release from a commitment they'd never made?

"We did have a good time at the beach, didn't we, Cary?" said Justin. "The three of us."

Cary put on an amazed expression. "Are you thinking of a *menage a trois*, my good doctor?"

Justin blushed as if Cary had overstepped the boundary of good taste. "I—no! Now you're being perverse. Probably this enforced idleness."

He sounded so pompous, so like her elderly family physician, that Cary grinned wickedly and touched his knee lightly. Justin moved just slightly away from her touch.

"Lighten up, Justin," she said. "I'm teasing. It's one of my perversities."

Justin ran his fingers through his hair. "I don't quite know where I stand with you, Cary."

"Do you need to, Justin?"

"Denise—"

"You and Denise don't need to worry about me, Justin," Cary interrupted gently. "I think you two might very well be perfect for each other."

"Denise doesn't want to hurt you, and we have been seeing a lot of each other." He seemed to run out of words.

Cary had an image of Denise sending Justin back to ThymeTable with an ultimatum: find out if Cary wants you. Quite fiery and determined in her own way, Denise would play fair only for a certain amount of time. Cary had seen Denise pursue, retreat, and pursue or stall in several contests over boys in college. She looked at Justin, now leaning back, eyes closed, basking in the sun even as he proclaimed he couldn't enjoy this environment for very long. He would certainly be a very wealthy physician, would work hard at being successful.

"Justin, I wish only the best for both of you," Cary said.

"Why don't you and Denise come down for a weekend soon? Maybe during the Herb Festival. Even if you don't want to live here, it is a nice place to visit!" Cary could have been a spokesperson for the Chamber of Commerce. "And you might want to keep your dad's place after all."

Justin opened his eyes. Cary saw his relief, relief that she was freeing him for his courtship. A courtship Cary felt sure was very much underway.

"No, I don't think so," he responded to Cary's last comment. "Maybe I always resented Dad's bringing me here. It was so arbitrary, and at time when I was too young to confer with, or so he thought. My roots are wherever my stethoscope is—"

"That's all? A stethoscope?" Cary prompted.

"And maybe where Denise is. Don't expect us to move too fast, Cary!"

"You're too reasonable and business-like, huh? I'm happy for you both."

Justin filled her in about Denise's rapidly growing business, in which clearly he took great pride. He jumped up. "Denise sent you a care package! I'll get it."

He returned with an elaborately wrapped basket filled with elegant soaps, bubble bath crystals, fancy hand towels, and lotions. At the end of the get-well note, Denise had added, "Enjoy—and pamper yourself. There's not an herbal anything in here!"

Cary exclaimed over everything and smelled deeply of the exquisite fragrances while Justin talked enthusiastically about his practice. Then he confided, "I've got a new car on order. It's a dark jade Jaguar, a real honey. I intended to get a black one, but Denise talked me into the jade. Not so doctorly she says. In a couple of months, I'll drive up in style!"

"Goodbye Volvo?"

"Yeah, goodbye Volvo. In fact, this weekend, I'm going to see if Johnny'll make me an offer. His girlfriend might like it. When's he getting married?"

"What in the world do you men know that I don't?" asked Cary. "Do you know for sure he's getting married?"

"He's got the ready look. It's just a matter of time. By Christmas, I'd say."

Cary gaped in surprise. She was going to look much more carefully at Johnny to try to discern just what these men saw that she didn't.

"Want to go up to the house with me?" said Justin. "To check on things in general, plumbing and moths in particular. I'll drive us up."

"Sure. I can hobble around the house, certainly well enough to watch you check on things! Alice and Agnes will likely want us to eat with them."

Justin grimaced. "Goat cheese, yum, yum."

As if to make up for his comment, Justin was especially charming to the Grayson sisters who promptly invited them to stop by for lunch. A couple of hours later, the two of them washed up and joined Alice and Agnes. The table was set with a delicious potato-chervil soup, rich and aromatic, one of their wonderful salads and goat cheese.

"This is fantastic," Justin complimented them. "I don't recognize half the green stuff in it, but it tastes great." He nibbled a leaf. "Nutty flavor."

"You'd think you'd have learned to recognize burnet," Agnes teased.

"And dandelion."

"And a touch of savory."

"And a tad of mint," finished Alice. The sisters beamed at Justin. They had watched him grow up, and they were proud him. They had always known that unless something extraordinary happened (like an eligible woman appearing on the scene) Justin would not stay close to the Cove.

"I did recognize the mint!" protested Justin. "I did."

"We'll give you the recipe, Cary," Agnes said. Then they

pressed Justin for details about his work, his apartment, his friends, and they obviously wanted to know about Denise. Within minutes, both sisters had sensed that whatever hopes they may have harbored, Cary and Justin were only good friends. A look had passed between the two sisters and they wisely kept quiet. Cary joined in the general conversation, but with a growing restlessness. It was mid-afternoon and frankly she longed to see Spence. After the interrupted non-kiss Thursday evening, she'd seen him only briefly. He had stuck his head in the door on his way to town the next morning when he had picked up several of her photographs to take in to Mark's studio. And again this morning he had time for only a quick cup of coffee before he adjusted her cushions and then hurried off. Dozens of little details about the festival had to be handled. Spence had enlisted Johnny and some of his buddies who were in and out of the greenhouses now, potting and repotting.

When Cary offered to assist by labeling or doing whatever she could, Spence responded sternly, "No. You don't need to be standing on your feet, Cary. The boys can take care of everything. Later I'll need your creative spirit," and he grinned, "and I don't want you worn to a frazzle as Agnes would say."

"Ready to go back to Rosemary?" Justin interrupted her reverie; she had been staring out the window. "Thanks a million for the wonderful lunch, girls." He gave each woman a peck on the cheek and a hug. Ugh, thought Cary, a tiny sliver of disapproval running through her, he's getting into the male superiority syndrome. I bet he calls all his older women patients girls, but the older men are sirs!

Justin wanted to visit colleagues in Asheville for the afternoon, possibly for dinner. In his hesitation, Cary realized he had been prepared to invite her to join him, would still do so if she gave any sign that she wanted his company.

"I'm a little tired, Justin," Cary told him, not untruthfully. "I'll see you before you leave tomorrow."

Spence's truck pulled into the drive at Rosemary within two minutes after Justin left. Sometimes there would be no traffic on the road for hours, Cary reflected, and now vehicles are all over the place.

Spence carried large pieces of Styrofoam which he dumped at Cary's feet. "Don't get up—not yet," he said, returning to his truck.

"Here are your pictures—blown up to gigantic proportions!" He pulled the chair closer to her, as Justin had done earlier. This time, however, Cary's pulse quickened and a warmness suffused her. Careful, she warned herself, fearing that her electrified senses would be evident. Spence held up, for her inspection, a four-by-four photograph of fuzzy spearmint. One drop of moisture hung tantalizingly from a leaf, so realistic-looking that anyone would want to stroke it, to crush it between fingertips.

"Wow!" Cary said. "It does look good. But Spence, these must have cost a fortune! Enlargements like this in color—"

"Not your problem, Cary. Mark charged me cost only—in return for crediting his studio in letters large enough for the public to see at forty feet! Look at this! This is the most sensual- looking budding basil I've ever seen. In fact, as much as I see these plants, I've never noticed them like this. Cary, you are wonderful. Ms. Photo-Herb!"

He held up another enlargement. "We only did four of these big ones. The others are in black and white—for closer viewing. Should we mat them or just stick them up with thumbtacks—for the quick and easy, casual look?"

"I can cut mats," Cary assured him, "although I may waste a little material at first. Matting with dark green will set them off, especially with a gray or beige backdrop."

"Lord, Ms. P-H," Spence said, "this is turning into a lot of work! For you—I mean!"

"For you. too, Spence. But we can spray paint the screens you built. I know they're practically finished."

At his quizzical look she went on, "No, I haven't been in your workshop. One of the boys mentioned it. You've been working late, huh?"

"I wanted to surprise you when they're finished," he admitted. "And they are now. The paint's dry. Are you working on comments or descriptions for the photos?" Spence seemed to suddenly remember something. "Or have you been otherwise engaged?"

"You saw Justin leaving?"

"We spoke briefly on the road. Has he been here long?"

"All morning. I think he definitely wants to sell his place. He's not at all interested in living here. We had a gourmet lunch with the sisters after some chores around his place." Cary was still engrossed in her photographs, mentally evaluating each one, noting what she might have done differently with lighting or cropping. She'd tell Spence about Denise and Justin later.

"Have you two got plans for tonight?" Spence studied a photograph at arm's length.

"My only plan for tonight is to write copy for these pictures. Justin's eating in town. I've thought about each one, but I don't know whether," she mused, "to go completely factual or to go legend-folklorish or to mix the two."

"Well," said Spence practically, "Why not put the words vertically? On the left, write something fanciful, and on the other side, put the facts."

"Great! That would work. Because some people want to know what an herb is good for exactly, and others like to know how the Romans or the Celts or their great-grandparents used the herb. We can get both! I'll have to work hard to keep from saying too much."

"Yeah, don't be too wordy. That's my English teacher-mother's advice. Say just enough."

"I can probably get about twenty-five or thirty words on

each side, depending on the type size. And Suzanne will do the lettering, the calligraphy."

Spence explained how he intended to hang the large prints with an ingenuous wiring scheme to prevent too much blowing in the breeze if there was a breeze. "You never can tell about the weather," he reminded Cary. "If we're lucky it'll be crisp, not too hot, a little wind but not much. A perfect blue sky like today. And we've been amazingly lucky the last few years."

"How many booths or vendors will there be?"

"Thirty or so," Spence told her. "Some larger farms have two areas. You'll like these people, Cary. As they say, I've never met an herbalist I didn't like. Their enthusiasm is contagious. I want to introduce you to them. Some have asked about my tenant. And there will be various demonstrations using herbs in a section set up by the agricultural extension people."

"Like what?"

"Oh, how to maintain an herb garden. I did that talk one year, but this time I'm not doing any demonstrating. Cooking with herbs. Treatments for pets. And how to make herb vinegars, various herbal remedies. I've tried to get the Grayson sisters involved, but they're fairly reticent about their concoctions."

"Not to me."

"To the public anyway. And there'll be special soaps and wreaths, all kinds of things. Chances are, you'll be asked to talk herb photography next year!"

"Next year—"

"Let's get this stuff indoors. Our famous changeable weather is about to do its thing." The sky had darkened without Cary even noticing, so engrossed was she in the nearness of Spence. A cool breeze brought goose pimples to her bare arms or else his presence gave her skin a tingly feeling. Spence pulled her to her feet. For an instant they stood very close.

It was Spence who stepped back, and he overturned the lawn chair. He quickly bent to retrieve it and laughed at his clumsiness. Cary too was glad the moment was over; she knew she would have melted, complete with goose pimples, into his arms at the slightest invitation.

"I've got to help the boys for awhile, til dark anyway," Spence told her. "Then I'll fix us an omelet or something simple—your place or mine after that. If you don't have other plans—"

"No plans except to write copy. But I could get us something to eat. You'll be tired."

"The guys'll be doing most of the work. And, no, you shouldn't stand too long yet on your foot."

"I'm okay—" Cary started.

"That I know. But you want to be at your best for the festival and not overextend yourself now. I can certainly throw together something that's edible."

"Mr. Beta man," Cary murmured, thinking of an article she'd read recently about the "new, gentle, caring" hero, so-called "beta" man. As she'd read she'd mentally placed Spence in the beta man role.

"What?"

"Nothing. I'd be delighted to have you cook for us at Rosemary. I've got all the fixings for an omelet or stir-fry." Cary wondered whether the evening would be all eating and business—all eggs and herbs. She gave her hair a shake. "I'll go shampoo my hair. I always think better with a clean head!"

Spence grinned, his arms loaded with foam board, "And Cary, please don't wear those bunny slippers. They do something for me and I can't be responsible for my actions!"

Cary mentally blessed her mother for those silly shoes. She giggled and threw a cushion at him.

The casualness about both Cary and Spence that evening fooled neither of them. Cary had soaked in a warm bath almost an hour, luxuriating in Denise's gift of foamy, fragrant bubble bath. She put on a long cotton skirt that fell gracefully to her ankles. She looked with some regret at the fuzzy bunny house shoes as she slipped her feet into soft moccasins. She would certainly do without her cane for the evening. She brushed on makeup and added just a bit of mascara. She decided she did not need blush, but she chose lipstick a little darker than usual. She knew she looked healthy, happy, and—in love? Did she look like a girl ready to seduce or ready to be seduced? She wrinkled her nose at her reflection in the mirror. Definitely she looked more alluring than she had in that tee shirt and bunny shoe! Now if only Spence thought so too.

Spence hadn't taken a bubble bath but his face was recently shaven. Cary didn't recognize the fragrance that wafted by her on his entrance, but she liked its fresh, masculine scent. Probably his secret herbal concoction, she thought wryly, but whatever it is, it's enticing. He had also changed into trousers of a muted gray cotton with a multicolored shirt of bright, broad stripes.

"I brought what I need for my special quiche," he announced, putting a cloth-covered basket on the table. "This will take a while, so we can have some wine once I get started."

In very short order he had rolled out dough and lined a pan with it; he then covered the dough with aluminum foil. Cary would never have thought that a man's floury fingers could be so sensuous. To distract herself, she asked, "What in the world are you making?"

"You'll see." Spence dumped handfuls of uncooked beans into the pan.

"We're not having baked beans in a quiche?" Cary teased. She forgot she intended to act alluring and had her chin propped in her hand as she leaned on the counter watching him work.

"This is Alice's special dish," Spence told her. "She insisted I make it tonight. She'll give you the recipe. This is only the second time I've done it, but it's simple enough."

A pang of jealously shot through the watching Cary. He'd probably made it for someone special. He'd probably made it the first time for Darla. Was she going to be forever in second place to Darla?

"Let me toss us a salad and then we can have some wine while we wait."

They carried their glasses into the living room. Spence promptly put his feet on the trunk that served as the coffee table. Then he just as quickly removed them.

"Go ahead," Cary said. "Make yourself at home. My home is your home!"

"I do almost forget that you're renting the place, Cary."

She gestured again for him to be comfortable, and he leaned back on the sofa, his feet on the table.

"I almost forget it too," she admitted.

Spence raised his glass in a toast, "Here's to the country—and to the almost-country woman!"

"What do you mean, almost?" She clinked her glass against his.

"Well, you have come a long way since you wandered in stepping all over the thyme," Spence said. "And the tart I'm making has thyme in it—a celebration of your arrival."

"And of my leaving?" Cary raised her eyebrows.

"Oh, I hope you'll stay around," he paused, "at least through the festival and the two months on our bet. Living on a farm isn't the most exciting life for everyone."

"Drudgery, drudgery," Cary drawled. "It certainly beats the nine-to-five routine I was into." She closed her eyes for a moment. Barrymore seemed far in the past. "Actually I liked my job and I was good at it, but now it seems another lifetime away."

"Same with me," Spence said. "Certainty is one thing, a

steady paycheck has lots of advantages. Not that 'certainty' was a sure thing there at the end, for me. I wonder if the business hadn't come unglued on me if I'd still be there, in a pleasant air-conditioned office, perfectly matched furniture, perfectly matched . . . girlfriend."

He paused briefly, then went on, "You know, Darla had found me, had returned to Ohio and looked me up. She wasn't very happy when I left the company. Even though I'd made no commitment and she continued to see other guys, she thought I was selfish, actually stupid to throw it all away to come out here. She made a big scene, a nasty scene."

Spence took a sip of wine. "Maybe I owe her something. Because she was so sure I'd come back, I determined to stay and make a success of this farm. Then I went home to celebrate my parents' golden anniversary. She came on strong. We spent one night together, as she put it, for old times' sake."

When Cary said nothing, Spence continued, "Then she came here. She swore she'd changed, she loved the idea of being a farmer's darling, she wanted to live in a rural area, to muck around in jeans, to 'smell the roses,' etc., and I was getting lonely, maybe."

Spence shook his head as if to clear it. "You don't want to hear this—"

"Yes, I do," Cary said. I need to hear it, she thought to herself. What did you owe Darla? "I was a fool. A major fool," Spence stated. "Darla played the perfect part." He sipped his wine. "She said she was pregnant, said I was the father, that she had not been seeing anyone. I believed her. Then in a couple of months, she took off. She'd put a lot of stuff on my credit cards. She took my car. Hell, she even took Max with her. She called. I was frantic with worry. Said she lost the baby, that she realized very soon that the farmer's life wasn't for her. She needed money, she said, for the hospital costs. I sent her my savings—most of it."

Cary wanted desperately to hold him, to caress away the grim lines that now etched his face. No wonder he didn't want to trust a woman.

"I felt so responsible, yet she wouldn't tell me where she was. I didn't know until the charges appeared on the phone bill the next month, and by then she wasn't at that number. I imagined her sick and alone, and needing money."

Spence laughed—a harsh sound against the soft Appalachian dulcimer music in the background. "That day—that day you fell, Darla came back again. This time she claimed she wanted to tell me the truth. There had been no baby. She was never pregnant. She was playing games, wanted to see if she'd like it here, and she knew I wouldn't throw her out if she announced she was carrying my child. And when she realized that living out here wasn't her cup of tea—horrible pun—she left. Now she's going to Europe with some guy from Detroit. Couldn't leave without telling me the truth. The truth is, she did lose Max. He was hit by a car. It was that grief I heard over the phone. She was crying. She did seem to be in pain. Over Max, my collie, not my baby."

Cary breathed deeply—uncertain of what to say. "Did you want a baby so badly?"

"Lord, no! I mean—Darla wasn't really the mothering type. She surprised me with the so-called news and I accepted it as fact. She kept planning, she said, to find a local doctor, and she was healthy enough. I thought she'd want to get married, but she kept postponing any decision about that too. Maybe that should have made me suspicious. I was a fool to not see through her."

Spence took a last gulp of wine. "Her farmer fool she called me the other day. She sees it all as a big joke. And she thinks I should be grateful. Well, I am in lots of ways. The only thing she's sorry about is losing Max. She did get attached to him."

Cary sat almost stunned, her mind reeling. Finally she

looked straight at Spence and said quietly, "Thank you for telling me."

"You had to know," Spence replied brusquely. He stood up. "And the shell should be baked. I'll put the rest of the meal together."

Cary stayed in her chair, grateful to be left alone to absorb Spence's story. Was he truly over Darla? He'd never said he loved her but her appeal must have been strong. Now what? She loved this man; of this she was sure, but was he ready to believe her, to trust her?

During the meal, Cary forced herself to move the fork with enthusiasm to her mouth. She complimented Spence on his culinary skill. She sipped her wine sparingly. Whatever the outcome of the evening, it had to be accomplished without the help of any alcoholic stimulus. As she dawdled over her food and kept up a superficial conversation, inwardly she faced reality: she wanted Spence, she wanted to make love to him. She hoped he could not see what she felt were clear signals emanating from her very being. If desire gave off sound waves, the room would be clanging from the vibrations.

Cary at some point realized that Spence now appeared subdued. He probably thought she didn't like his cooking. The tart even with its wonderful aroma and hint of thyme could only be discussed so much. An outsider looking in the window would have been reminded of shy teenagers on their first date, on prom night, each wondering just what the next move would be.

The tension grew in Cary. When Spence had cleared the table with an affable but strained smile and had settled on the sofa while the coffee was making, Cary decided to throw caution to the wind.

She sat down next to him. He turned his face toward her, surprised at just how close she had placed herself to him. Without a word, she took his face in both her hands and kissed him. His lips parted in response and Cary pursued her advantage. She'd never played the serious aggressor—the outright aggressor before, and she'd intended a quick kiss to see what his reaction would be. Spence gasped for a breath of air and broke the immediate intensity. "Now," he said huskily, "Let's try that again." Before the words were finished, they were lost in a long kiss that left both of them shaken.

For a moment Cary was tempted to draw back, to joke about the situation—for just a moment. Then her eyes closed and she leaned, merged into Spence's chest. She didn't want to see his face yet. Her desire was a flame melting her, melding her to him. She slipped her hand into his shirt and he shivered with pleasure.

Spence spoke, into her neck, as his hand moved along her thigh. "Cary, Cary, if you're sorry for me, don't do something you'll regret later. I don't want your sympathy."

Cary said, "Sympathy is not what I'm feeling at the moment." She kissed the hollow of his neck, tracing her tongue downward. "The truth is—I want you—more than anything in the world. And I want you now."

"Here, here's the glass of water you requested, madam." Spence stood naked at the edge of the bed, faintly visible in the moonlight. "And I brought us coffee. No use letting good coffee go to waste!"

Cary propped a pillow behind her head. She'd forgotten that Spence had put coffee on just before she'd begun her seduction of him. In fact, she'd forgotten everything in the lovemaking that she initiated and that Spence had entered into so wholeheartedly. "Thanks," she murmured. "Wow, it's strong!"

"Been sitting there awhile," Spence grunted, as he

managed to snuggle under the sheet without spilling a drop of the coffee from the cup in his hand. "Just think, we could have had the coffee fresh—or—" He kissed her shoulder, his lips warm and damp.

"If I hadn't practically forced myself on you, Spence!" Cary was drowsy, languid; yet she felt a tiny pang from her ladylike past. She held the cup in both hands, keeping her eyes downward as she took a sip. "Oh, I'm embarrassed. Believe me, such is not my normal behavior."

"I believe you, I suppose," Spence teased. "But you certainly have the technique down pat." He reached over and turned on a bedside lamp. "I want you—and I want you now!"

He chuckled at the blush that reddened Cary's face. "I had to see your expression," he explained, gesturing toward the light, "and now I want to see all of you."

"Well, I am embarrassed," Cary repeated, sighing deeply. "A little. But I'm not one bit sorry."

Yes, she had with clear intentions started the lovemaking, but Spence had lost no time in responding and taking over. After a moment when he seemed a little amused and then amazed, he had kissed Cary until she was breathless. When his exploring hands had elicited moans of desire from her, he'd picked her up from the sofa and carried her into the bedroom. At first their undressing had been slow, deliberate. Then their passion had accelerated so that now clothes were strewn all over the room.

"Then finish that coffee," Spence directed gruffly. He set his mug on the table and took Cary's cup from her willing hands. His tone softened, "Because I want you—and I want you now."

He pulled her to him, his hands running down her back, sending delicious shivers of warmth through her.

"Well, prove it, mister," Cary challenged. And he did.

When Cary awakened, Spence was not beside her. For a long time she lay dreamily remembering their passion.

Never before had she given so freely and yet felt so utterly consumed. Yet in her cries of release and in the quiet moments that followed when she lay entangled in Spence's arms, and, she knew, ensnared completely in her heart, she had not let herself say, "I love you." She did love him, of that she had no doubt. Why hadn't she told him? What held her back? Was he still in Darla's thrall? Cary didn't think so. But he was disillusioned about her deception. He wasn't ready, most likely, to give his heart—as easily as he'd given his body—to another woman. Cary yawned and stretched prodigiously. She counseled herself that she could love Spence and leave him free of commitments. She hugged his pillow to her face, breathing deeply of his smell and reveling in remembering the night.

Coffee was made in the kitchen. Cary smiled again. Spence had left a note. "Business calls. And I'll call later."

Cary ate a hearty breakfast of eggs and toast with Mrs. Alison's homemade elderberry jelly. She read the attached recipe as if it were a love poem. As she puttered about, writing the herbal commentary for the festival, she quoted, "My love is like a red red rose . . ."

When Spence did call, however, she heard none of the softness of a lover's voice. He sounded very much the businessman. "Cary, can you get most of the copy done by tomorrow? We're going to be meeting here all day to go over the plans for the layout of the booths, all that sort of thing. I'll be in touch but it'll be tomorrow most likely."

"Sure," Cary tried to match his businesslike tone. "I'm working on the copy now. Suzanne may come by later and we can get started on the calligraphy."

She heard Spence yell to someone "Just a minute," before he spoke into the receiver, "Thanks, Cary. You're great."

"I—" Cary almost gulped in her disappointment at his impersonal tone. Then she said resolutely, "You too." And she hung up, leaving him, she hoped, to wonder at her comment. And when Spence seemed determined to avoid her during the coming days, she masked her disappointment by working diligently with Suzanne to perfect the posters and by wandering in the early mornings and late afternoon sun to catch the light for more photographs. Fate seemed to conspire against any privacy for her and Spence and she began to think he helped fate along by slipping away just before they could be alone. He apparently never planned to be alone with her again. But Cary still wasn't sorry she had seduced him; even if she now had his scorn, even if he found her too aggressive. However, she had little time to dwell on Spence's aloofness.

ThymeTable Farm became a virtual beehive of activity— with visitors arriving in a flurry.

First came Cary's parents, Ruthlene and David Randall. They drove up to Rosemary Cottage without warning. Ruthlene had become worried. Cary had been adamant about being "fine," yet Ruthlene detected something different in her daughter's voice. She had called her husband at work. "I'll have your bag packed. We're going to western North Carolina to visit Cary. Something's not right, I can just tell." David Randall knew that, business or no business, his wife meant what she said. He hurried to have the car serviced.

It was midmorning when they arrived. Perhaps influenced by Phillip's description they expected the worse and were surprised to see Cary scrubbed and serene at the kitchen table mulling over recipes in an herb cookbook.

"Mother! Dad! What a surprise!" Cary welcomed them with hugs and kisses.

"We had to come see for ourselves just how you're doing." Ruthlene held Cary's hands and backed off an arm's length to get a better look.

"Oh, Mother, I am fine. I told you. Now I'll show you."

Cary laughed, "See, my bruises are practically gone. I'm walking fine—in my hightops. Come on, I'll show you the farm."

Cary introduced her parents to Mary and the Grayson sisters who insisted on feeding them a lunch of goat cheese and vegetable casserole. Spence was in Asheville according to Mary, who also had errands to run in town. During the rest of the day the Randalls saw that Cary was indeed healthy and happy at ThymeTable. Ruthlene noticed a certain withdrawal whenever Spence's name was mentioned, but she also noticed Cary's pride in the farm. She had amassed an amazing amount of knowledge about herbs in the short time she'd been here, and Ruthlene wondered about her motive.

"I can put you up here, Mother." Cary looked around, "You can have the bedroom and I'll take the sofa. I know it's good for sleeping." But her parents insisted on returning to Asheville to spend the next few days, promising to visit each day if they weren't in the way.

At ten o'clock the next morning, Cary looked up from her work to see Spence ready to knock on the door. Her heart leaped with joy, then plummeted. He looked very business-like in a light gray suit and conservative tie.

"Cary, I've got to meet some bankers to straighten out a few things, and then—" he was interrupted by the Randalls pulling into the driveway.

Cary made the introductions. Her father and mother shook hands with Spence who repeated that he had to rush into town for a meeting.

Chapter 12

"Darling, you can still make a fortune on this place. We can live anywhere—wherever you want." It was Darla's voice. Cary knew it in an instant, the same sultry quality, only intensified, that she had heard when Darla had called about Spence.

Cary halted just as she was about to push open the door of the shed-like attachment to the greenhouse. Her heart seemed to thud like a lump to her toes. Darla! She was supposed to be somewhere with her new boyfriend. Yet here she was, sounding so sure of herself, so persuasive. In spite of all he had told her, was it possible that Spence was thinking of selling? Cary's first impulse was to slink out unseen, to hurry back to Rosemary where her parents were resting, to disappear completely. A temporary paralysis kept her rooted to the spot, her hand on the doorknob.

"Darla," Spence's voice grated in the stillness. "You have more nerve than I ever gave you credit for. And I gave you credit for a lot of it! You can't be serious."

"I'm very serious, my love. With my influence, Phillip Randall will almost double his offer. I guarantee it. With the up-front money and your investment skills, you'd be a millionaire. We could—"

Cary breathed deeply and stepped into the room, letting the door close quietly behind her. Spence and Darla both swung around at the sound.

Darla hand rested lightly on Spence's arm. Rather than drop it, she tightened her fingers on the fabric of his shirt. Spence, however, stepped away abruptly. Darla covered the awkward moment as her arm dropped by gazing at Cary as though she were a lost bovine who had wandered into the room.

"It's Cary, isn't it?" She spoke first. "Spence's new tenant."

"Let me introduce—" Spence said. Instinctively he moved toward Cary. She ignored him, her eyes upon the woman who was intent at this moment on destroying Cary's world.

"And you're Darla," Cary returned. Darla was every bit as beautiful as Cary had imagined, more striking than the camera had shown that day at See-Off. In her pale linen slacks topped by a silk shirt and mauve scarf, she could have stepped directly from a page of a fashion magazine.

"And you've been in contact with Phillip and Alecia? You'd like to see ThymeTable and the all this land turned into a golf course, wouldn't you? You could probably finagle the biggest house on the eighteenth hole as part of the bargain. Could you bear to live here at least part of the year? Would that be too demanding? Right where the thyme bed is would be the perfect spot, wouldn't it? Near the pool, close to the tennis courts, you could have your own recreational complex. Everything you—" Cary's eyes blazed and her cheeks were flushed. As she turned the image in her mind into words, her words came tumbling out, almost incoherent.

Taken aback at the outburst, Darla stared at the girl whom she saw as simply an intruder, a mere money-paying guest. She knew Cary rented Rosemary, but now she realized Cary might be more than just a temporary tenant. Her eyes narrowed, and her voice turned silky. "I don't think the idea of the farm becoming a condo complex could fuel your anger, charming though it is. Surely it's more than that. Don't tell me you've fallen for Spence!"

Darla stopped, then went on, "Spence and I go back a long way."

"And I've been here a short time," Cary said. "But I care about this farm, this cove, and yes, I care—"

"Care about Spence!" Darla almost crowed in triumph. "Oh, my dear man," she turned toward him. "Another little one worshiping at your feet."

"I'm not in your league," Cary said defiantly. "Spence was clear about that. And now that I see you, I believe it. But Darla, I don't want to play in your league. You'd sell out something your man loves—for money, to indulge yourself. You're a self-serving—"

"Hold it, hold it!" Spence stepped between the two women. Cary was glaring. Darla was coolly appraising her. In another moment Cary would have attacked, if her tightly clinched fists were any indication.

"Cary, believe me. I didn't expect Darla here today—or any day. I thought she was gone. Now it appears that somewhere along the way, the Pullmans got in touch with her. And she volunteered—" Spence's voice was scathing.

Darla appeared unmoved. She said sweetly, "Can I smoke in here? I need a cigarette."

"Volunteered to come down to Asheville and meet with your brother, to see if she could help me decide." Spence leaned against a waist-high table, almost in wonderment. "Ah, Darla, we do go back a long way, and I've been a slow learner. But somehow, I think you have been even slower—if you really believe you can now influence me. In any direction."

Spence shook his head. "Let's go outside if you must smoke." He tried to catch Cary's eye as the three of them moved toward the door, but Cary, almost shaking in anger, had turned and stalked out first.

"Cary, let me explain," he said. "When I talked to Pullman one day, he said something about Phillip's letting drop a comment about a sort of 'secret weapon' in the dealing about ThymeTable and the Cove. And then when he used the word 'she' I naturally assumed he meant you. I'm sorry about misjudging you. It—"

"You thought and you accused, Spence Bradford! You thought I, your little one worshiping at your feet, you thought I . . ." Cary flung the words out, uncertain where they were going. "Well, I won't let ThymeTable be turned into a golf course! If Darla can get Phillip to double his offer, I-I can do better. I'll buy the farm myself."

"You?" Darla flicked ash from her cigarette, amused. "I thought you worked at some little college somewhere."

"Cary, wait a minute!" Spence shouted. "Damn it, the farm isn't for sale. The Cove isn't for sale. I don't know what Darla has told Phillip, but remember Jon is going to take over the Cove with a sort of land trust. Darla came today to make one last effort, a last-ditch stand." He turned to Darla, who was looking at Cary with a kind of bemused admiration at her intensity.

"Darla, please leave. The ties are cut. The strings are gone. Don't embarrass yourself by being asked twice to get off this property. I've seen my banker. Everything's cleared up. You don't have access to any accounts and you know it. You've done all the financial damage you can do here." Spence's face was flushed but his words were ice-cutting cold.

"Spence, darling, are you sure about what you're saying?" Darla spoke with the intimacy of the bedroom. "Give me a chance to explain."

"And any other damage has been cured long since." Spence's finality would have chilled anyone less assured than Darla.

"If you say so." She ground out her cigarette with a quick twist of her shoe. "But if ever you need to dash off, look me up! We had some good times."

She turned toward the door and smiled. "William is waiting at the Radisson. We're off to New York and then to Paris. Still, it was worth a chance. I promised Phillip I'd make a real effort. I'll report failure and wish you luck with this place." She looked around with scorn. "You'll surely need it. Bye now."

She could have been modeling on a runway, so smooth were her steps toward her car on the other side of the farmhouse.

Spence stared at her back. Cary stared at the ground.

"Cary—" he began.

"I meant it, you know." Cary said quietly. "I'd do anything to keep ThymeTable a farm. With my trust fund and what I could borrow from my parents, I could make a down payment."

"Or you could marry the owner," Spence said, "and keep the farm that way."

"You—you! I wouldn't marry you just to keep the farm!"

"You said you'd do anything—" Spence reminded her, his face a blank.

"Is this a private marriage proposal?" a voice asked from the doorway. "Or can anyone put in a bid?"

"Jon!" Spence stuck out his hand, and then the two men hugged briefly. "What timing, old friend! It's great to see you."

Cary took the interruption time to calm herself down. She unclenched her fingers and told herself to breathe deeply, to get a grip, to take care in what she said. She looked with interest at Jon, Jon the drifter, the forgetful parent, the creative spirit, Johnny's dad, Mary's ex-husband. If she had been required to put her imagining of him on paper, she would have drawn a tall, weathered, Jack London type. Instead Jon resembled her idea of an overgrown leprechaun.

He was only a few inches taller than Cary and he was rotund. His thinning hair was long, curling up on his shirt collar and his eyes twinkled with humor. The belt stretched across his ample girth was obviously fine hand tooled leather and he wore an earring with leather threads and beads.

"Cary!" he boomed. He embraced her warmly and then stood back to nod his approval. "Luckily you don't have to hock the family jewels to save this place," he laughed. "And you don't have to marry the jilted owner either! Forgive me, Spence, but I met Darla as I pulled in—we almost bashed each other. I gather she'd gone again. For good this time."

Jon threw up his arms. "This place is getting as crowded as downtown Asheville on a Bele Chere day," Jon went on. "Cars everywhere! A few days and I'll be on my way. But I didn't want to miss the festival this year. And I have some business details to work out with Mary."

"Come on over to the house, Jon, and have some coffee," Spence invited. "We've all got business details to work out. Have you seen Mary and Johnny?"

"They're out, according to the sisters. I hear Johnny's getting married pretty soon!"

Cary felt dazed. "I-I'll be getting back to Rosemary," she said. "Mom and Dad are there."

The men protested. Wouldn't she join them? She shook her head and trudged toward her cottage. She needed some time to think. She'd seduced Spence shamelessly and enjoyed their lovemaking beyond her wildest dreams. Now she had as much as tried to buy him, certainly to buy his farm. Naturally he felt compelled to propose. What kind of woman was she turning into?

Cary grinned. She was exactly what she wanted to be and where she wanted to stay. When she entered the living room where her parents were contentedly leafing through her books and chatting aimlessly. They looked up, "It certainly is peaceful here, Cary."

Cary plopped herself down beside her mother and hugged her. "Ah, Mother! It's not that peaceful! Just now I have routed the one woman I've ever wanted to punch in the nose. And I've just met Jon the leprechaun, and—" she decided to go the whole route, "I've just made it clear that I'd buy this farm if I have to."

Cary grinned wickedly at her Dad's amazed look. "Would you have loaned me a few thou, Dad? To keep ThymeTable out of Phillip's hands?"

"Punch somebody—" her mother exclaimed.

"Loan you a few thousand?" her dad sputtered. All three broke into laughter. Although baffled at this confident Cary, her parents hadn't seen Cary so animated and sparkling in months, even years.

"ThymeTable agrees with you, Cary." Her mother beamed.

"Go for it," her dad said. "Phillip's got other fish to fry, other land to develop." When her father spoke so informally and unreservedly, Cary knew he was happy. He usually kept his language fairly formal and restrained. "Go for it" said far more than just the words. He was issuing his complete approval.

"David," said Ruthlene, with asperity.

"Yes, dear?"

"Don't just sit there. How much do you need, Cary? How many thousands?"

"Oh, Mother, I don't really need any. But thanks. Things are working out. Spence will keep the farm and Jon will rescue the cove." Cary laughed. "And I am going to stay on, here in Rosemary. It's where I'm happiest."

"Not in Rosemary, you don't." Spence spoke from the doorway. Jon stood just behind him.

"What?" Cary stammered. "I can't stay on in Rosemary?"

Spence's face was unreadable. He introduced Jon to the Randalls. Then he stood looking at Cary. "Nope, not in Rosemary."

"Spence Bradford! I have paid my rent through the month! You—you landlord!"

The Randalls looked at Cary, worried; then they looked at Spence whose eyes took on a devilish sparkle.

"Cary, you little adorable fool. I can't seem to get a moment alone with you. I give up. So here in front of your mother and dad, in front of Jon, I'm asking you: will you marry me? Will you live in the big house with me? Will you take ThymeTable Farm for better or worse. In short, will you give up your lease on Rosemary?"

Cary paled and then she blushed. She wanted to jump up and kiss Spence until he wiped that silly grin off his face. She wanted to shout to the mountains her love. But for a few seconds she was speechless although her eyes spoke volumes.

Spence dropped to his knee before her—while her parents and Jon looked on. "I'll make it poetic, darling. Come live with me and be my love and we will all love's pleasures prove."

Cary turned to her mother, her eyes bright with happiness. "His mother's an English teacher. We'll probably quote each other to death."

Not positive, in spite of the glow on her daughter's face, that Cary should be placed into such a public declaration of intentions, Ruthlene said, "Cary, don't you need—"

Her Dad was saying at the same time, "There are lots of things you need—"

They were interrupted by both Cary and Spence—and Jon declaring loudly, "Oh reason not the need!"

Cary leaned forward and kissed Spence on the forehead. "Let's go somewhere more private," she murmured. "I've never been proposed to in a room full of people."

Spence took her hand, pulled her to her feet, and picked her up easily. He looked out the window. "Oh my god, the room's going to get more crowded! Here comes your brother and his wife!"

"Let's get out of here! I'll be back later. Mom, you entertain Phillip."

Spence carried Cary down the steps as Phillip and Alecia got out of the car. Cary heard her mother calling out to her, "But we don't know your answer, Cary!"

David Randall said, "We don't?"

A few minutes later Spence enveloped Cary in his arms as they stood in his kitchen. "Oh, my darling Cary," he said, "I'm getting in the habit of carrying you around. I knew I was captured that first day you arrived. Do you know your answer yet?"

Cary tightened her arms around Spence. "I do have one question, Spence. Is she truly gone? Is Darla truly gone?"

"Gone forever. And has been. Even today, she was playing a game, seeing if I'd play. You heard her. She had William waiting at the hotel. I knew when she followed me here that if we married it would be for the wrong reason. She knew it too or she wouldn't have lied about a baby."

Spence ran his lips over Cary' face and neck, breathing softly near her ear. "And you? Cary, do you have any question about yourself?"

"Not one. I love you with a passion—I'm so flustered I can't remember the rest of that quotation." She kissed him.

"We can get married during or after the festival if that's not too soon, Cary."

Then Spence slapped his forehead. "I'm being inconsiderate. Will you, or your mother, want a big Barrymore wedding? Or," he grinned provocatively, "We can just dash off to some exotic spot. Whatever you want. But let's make it soon."

"Dash off! With all these herbs to be taken care of? I want to be married right after the festival, right here on the farm," Cary declared. "With herbs to the right of me, herbs to the left of me."

"Goat cheese at the reception?" Spence grinned. "Definitely."

Later as she lay with her head in his lap, she said, "I'm going to ask Denise and Alecia to be bridesmaids, and Mary can be my matron. Can you get along with Phillip? He'll have to give up looking after me. That might be hard for him."

"No problem. I can talk business with him, give him some good arguments about mixing investments and environmental concerns. He may never approve of your marrying a farmer, though."

"I love my farmer, Cary said firmly. "For all seasons and for all T-H-Y-M-E."

Cary's Collection of Recipes

Cream of Barley Soup

½ cup of barley, soaked overnight or several hours
1 onion, diced
2 stalks of celery, sliced thin
1 cup tomato juice or vegetable juice
1 carrot, diced
1 teaspoon of salt or to taste
1 cup of vegetable consomme or stock
1½ quarts of water

Drain the soaked barley. Add the water, onion, carrot, celery, and salt. Bring to a boil and immediately reduce heat. Cover and simmer until barley is tender. Add tomato/vegetable juice and vegetable consomme/stock. Blend in blender until smooth.

Mrs. Alison's Oatmeal Molasses Bread

8 cups flour
1 ½ cups quick-cooking rolled oats
3/4 cup molasses
1/4 cup lukewarm water
1 cake fresh yeast
2 tsp. salt
1 quart of milk
1/4 cup vegetable shortening

Cook oats in milk about 10 minutes, stirring constantly. Add the molasses, salt, and shortening. Cool to lukewarm and add yeast (dissolved in the 1/4 cup water). Work in all the flour and turn onto a lightly floured board. Knead until smooth (10 minutes or so). Place in greased bowl, cover and let rise in a warm, draft-free place until double in bulk. Punch down, divide into thirds and shape into three loaves. Place in greased pans and let rise until nearly doubled.

Bake at 400 degrees for 10 minutes; reduce heat to 375 and bake 40 minutes longer. Remove from pans. Brush with butter and cool.

Elderberry Jelly

2 cups elderberry juice
2 cups apple juice
3 cups of sugar

Combine the juices and bring to a boil. Add the sugar gradually, stirring. Cook rapidly until jelly slides off the edge of a spoon. Remove from heat. Pour into hot, sterilized jars. When the jelly is cooled and set, seal with paraffin and screw on lids.

Cary's Omelet

1/3 cup chopped onions
1/3 cup chopped green pepper
2 Tablespoons butter
1 Tablespoon oil
½ cup Swiss (or your preference) cheese
3 eggs, beaten
½ teaspoon salt or to taste
½ to 1 cup noodles, cooked

Melt 1 tablespoon of butter and oil in pan. Saute the onion and green peppers until the onion begins to brown. Stir in the other tablespoon of butter and all other ingredients. Cook ten or more minutes until the omelet is slightly puffed, browned around the edges and firm to the touch. Sprinkle with extra cheese if desired.

Spence's Simple Eggplant Casserole

Preheat oven to 350 degrees

Combine in a bowl:

15 saltine crackers and 2 Tablespoons melted butter

Toss. Remove 1/4 cup to use for topping.

Add to the remaining crumbs:

3 cups cubed eggplant

½ cup shredded cheddar cheese

1/4 cup chopped celery

½ teaspoon of salt and 1/4 teaspoon of pepper

1 cup evaporated milk

Put into a greased casserole dish. Top with reserved breadcrumbs.

Bake 45 minutes.

ThymeTable Brownies

1/3 cup of butter—melted
1 cup brown sugar
1 egg
½ teaspoon salt
3/4 cup sifted flour
1 teaspoon baking powder
½ teaspoon cinnamon
2/4 teaspoon vanilla
½ cup coconut
1 6-ounce package chocolate chips
½ cup chopped black walnuts or pecans

Stir together melted butter, brown sugar, egg, salt, baking powder, flour and vanilla. Mix well and add the coconut, chocolate chips, and nuts. Spread in a greased 9-inch square pan. Bake at 350 degrees for 25 minutes

Cary's Chilled Cucumber Soup

3 Tablespoons onion, minced fine
3 cups of milk
1/4 cup of butter
1 cup light cream
1/4 cup flour
3 large cucumbers, diced salt to taste (about 1 teaspoon)

Saute the onion in butter over low heat until transparent but not brown. Blend in flour and salt. Add the milk and cream, stirring constantly. Cook until the sauce is smooth and thickened. Remove from heat and add cucumbers. Puree in blender. Chill for an hour or so. Garnish with yogurt and dill as desired.

Suzanne's Sugar Cookies

1 cup sugar
½ cup shortening
2 eggs
2 Tablespoons milk
1 Tablespoon lemon extract
3 ½ cups flour
2 teaspoons baking powder

Cream sugar and shortening in a bowl until light and fluffy. Add eggs, milk, and lemon extract and beat well. Stir the flour and baking powder into the mixture. Cover and chill for an hour or so. Roll out on floured surface to about 1/4 inch thickness, and cut into rounds with a biscuit cutter or glass. Place on lightly greased cookie sheet. Bake at 375 degrees for 8 to 10 minutes. Sprinkle with sugar or a touch of cinnamon as desired.

Mrs. Alison's Special Buttermilk Pie

1 ½ cups sugar
½ cup buttermilk
1 Tablespoon flour a tad of salt (1/8 teaspoon)
½ cup melted butter
1 ½ teaspoon vanilla
3 eggs, well beaten

Combine the sugar and flour. Beat the eggs thoroughly. Add them and the other ingredients to the flour/sugar mixture and stir until smooth. Pour into an unbaked pie shell and bake at 350 degrees for approximately 45 minutes.

Alice's Quiche With a Touch of Thyme

1 deep 9-inch unbaked pastry shell
2-4 cups dried beans
½ cup chopped onion
½ cup chopped red bell peppers
2 Tablespoons vegetable oil
2 tomatoes, peeled and chopped
2 teaspoons basil, crushed
½ teaspoon salt and a dash of pepper
2 cups of milk
5 eggs
½ cup grated Swiss cheese
1 Tablespoon butter
½ teaspoon of thyme, crushed

Butter a large sheet of light weight aluminum foil; place buttered side down in the pastry shell, pushing foil gently up around the sides. Prick well. Fill completely with beans, any kind. Bake in a pre-heated 450 degrees oven for 10 minutes or until pastry is set. Remove the liner and bake another 2 to 3 minutes until the shell begins to shrink slightly from the edges of the pan. Remove from oven, let cool on rack.

Saute onion and pepper in oil until tender. Add the chopped tomatoes, basil, thyme, salt and pepper. Cover and simmer 5 minutes; uncover and cook until liquid is evaporated. Remove from heat. Beat together the milk and eggs. Put the tomato mixture in the pastry shell and pour the egg mixture over. Sprinkle with the grated cheese and dot with butter. Bake in pre-heated oven at 375 degrees until puffed and brown and knife inserted in the center is clean—35-40 minutes. Garnish with tomato slices and more basil.

ThymeTable's Tea to Sleep By

8 Tablespoons lemon thyme
2 Tablespoons lemon basil
½ teaspoon lemon balm
4 Tablespoons mild green tea
Use 1 teaspoon per cup, more or less to taste.

Cary's Tarragon and Thyme Cream Cheese Spread

8 ounces cream cheese, softened
½ teaspoon tarragon
1/4 teaspoon thyme
3 Tablespoons minced parsley

Mix thoroughly and let mellow for a couple of hours before serving.

The Grayson Sisters' Fresh Neufchatel Cream Cheese

Add one tablespoon of sour milk to a gallon of goat's milk at 72 degrees. Dissolve ½ of a junket tablet in 1/4 cup of cold water (be sure the water is cold) and stir into the milk. Start this cheese at night, and after 18 hours pour the curd into a muslin or unbleached cotton bag. Let the curd drain in a cool place for about 24 hours. When the curd is firm, add 1 ½ teaspoons of salt for each pound of cheese. Enjoy this cheese fresh.

The Grayson sisters' goat cheese (soft)

Weigh a gallon of goat's milk (it will weight around eight pounds). Heat one gallon of fresh goat's milk to 72 degrees. Add two tablespoons of fresh buttermilk and two drops of cheese rennet diluted in 1/4 cup of water. Stir the milk for approximately two minutes. Let it set at 72 degrees for eighteen to twenty hours. After the milk has set, pour the curd into a muslin bag. Hang the bag up in a cool place to allow drainage of whey. The whey will drain sufficiently in twelve to twenty-four hours, depending on the temperature. The lower the temperature of the cheese during the draining, the shorter the drainage time. When the cheese weighs slightly less than half the original weight, the drainage is complete. Salt the cheese to taste, usually about two teaspoons of salt per pound. Work the salt into the cheese and then refrigerate, for up to two weeks.